THE SPOOK'S BESTIARY

THE LAST APPRENTICE

THE SPOOK'S BESTIARY

THE GUIDE TO CREATURES Of THE DARK

JOSEPH DELANEY

Illustrated by Julek Heller

GREENWILLOW BOOKS

An Imprint of HarperCollinsPublishers

The Last Apprentice
The Spook's Bestiary: The Guide to Creatures of the Dark
Text copyright © 2010 by Joseph Delaney
Illustrations copyright © 2010 by Julek Heller

First published in 2010 in Great Britain by The Bodley Head, an imprint of Random House Children's Books, under the title *The Spook's Bestiary*. First published in 2011 in the United States in hardcover by Greenwillow Books; first Greenwillow Books paperback edition, 2014.

The text of this book is set in 11-point Palatino.

Library of Congress Cataloging-in-Publication Data
Delaney, Joseph, (date).
The Spook's Bestiary / by Joseph Delaney ; illustrations by Julek Heller.
"Greenwillow Books."
p. cm. — (The Last Apprentice)
Summary: Ready to be presented to the last apprentice, Tom Ward, the spook's notebook contains instructions for vanquishing boggarts, witches, the unquiet dead, and other dark creatures and spirits.
ISBN 978-0-06-208114-8 (trade bdg.) — ISBN 978-0-06-208115-5 (pbk.)
[1. Supernatural—Fiction. 2. Apprentices—Fiction. 3. Horror stories.]
I. Heller, Julek, illustrator. II. Title.
PZ7.D373183Sm 2011 [Fic]—dc22 2010049856

14 15 16 17 18 LP/RRDH 10 9 8 7 6 5 4 3

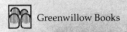
Greenwillow Books

To Marie—
J.D.

To Anne—
J.H.

CONTENTS

Mages

To the Reader

My name is John Gregory and I've
walked the length and breadth of the
County for more years than I care to
remember, defending it against ghosts,
ghasts, boggarts, witches, and all manner of
things that go bump in the night. The trade
I follow is that of a spook, and all those
who practice our craft must be the seventh
son of a seventh son, with the ability to see
and talk to the dead, and with a degree
of immunity against witches.

Each spook takes on and trains
apprentices so that the fight against
the dark may go on from generation to
generation. And an important part of
what we do is accrue, record, and share
knowledge so that we may learn from the
past. What follows is my Bestiary—my

personal account of the denizens of the dark
I've encountered, together with the lessons I
have learned and the mistakes I have made.
I have held nothing back, and my hope is
that the spook who follows me will continue
to keep this record of the practical ways in
which we deal with the dark.

The fight will go on, and there are always
new things to learn about our enemies—and,
indeed, new types of enemy to face. But we
must take heart from the fact that the record
shows we are always finding ways to deal
with each fresh threat. As long as I can see
and am able to hold a pen, I will continue to
augment this store of knowledge. Let this
Bestiary grow and be added to by each new
spook who follows my path.

John Gregory
of Chipenden

The Dark

The Dark

We can only speculate as to how the dark originated. Perhaps it was there from the moment the universe was first created, a force to balance against the light, each striving from that first instant to gain the upper hand. One other possibility is that it was a tiny seed of possibility that grew stronger as its roots developed and fed upon human wickedness. For there is no doubt in my mind that human involvement—especially the worship of and contact with the servants of the dark for personal gain—is strengthening it now.

Whatever the truth, the dark is still growing in power, and its denizens threaten to plunge the whole world into a long age of terror and bloodshed.

How to Deal with the Dark
(General preparations and remedies)

1. It is important to prepare the mind. To conquer one's fear is difficult, but that is the first thing that must be done. The dark feeds upon human fear, which enables it to grow stronger. It helps

to breathe slowly and deeply and focus on the task at hand. A spook must be prepared to die if necessary. Once that is accepted, the fear often fades into insignificance. Our duty to the County is more important than our own lives.

2. It is beneficial to fast: This clears the mind and makes us less susceptible to dark magic. However, a balance must be struck because our work is often physically demanding. When the dark threatens, I keep up my strength by eating very small pieces of County cheese.*

3. Fortunately there are many substances that cause pain and eventual destruction to the creatures of the dark—or, at the very least, limit their capacity to do harm. The combination of salt and iron is particularly effective against boggarts and witches and can be used either to slay or bind them. Rowan is the most effective wood against witches, and a

*I had not been working from the Chipenden house for long when I learned that the village and surrounding area are the very center of County cheese-making.—
John Gregory

I'm sick to death of eating cheese. For me it's the very worst part of the job. I don't know how much longer I can put up with it.—apprentice Andy Cuerden

Andrew Cuerden left within a month of making the above observation. This trade needs discipline. He thought too much about the needs of his belly and lacked commitment.—
John Gregory

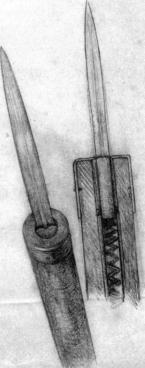

silver alloy can hurt even the most powerful of the dark's servants. Hence a spook's use of a rowan staff with a retractable silver alloy blade.

4. A silver chain, which can be used to bind a witch, is an equally useful tool. It is less effective against demons, but even there may temporarily incapacitate them until a blade can be used.

5. A spook's best weapons against the dark are common sense, courage, plus the acquisition of skills and knowledge built up over many generations. We don't use magic. Ours is a craft, a trade, and we must learn from both our mistakes and our successes.

An Angry Stone Chucker

BOGGARTS

Boggarts are far more numerous in the County than anywhere else on earth. There are several different types of these spirit entities—some are little more than an irritation, but others can cause serious damage to property, or to people, and in some cases they may even prove deadly.

Typically boggarts make their lairs in cellars, barns, and hollow trees; most are, at the very least, an inconvenience to people nearby. They are usually invisible, but unless exceptionally powerful, they can be seen by spooks. When angry or happy they briefly show themselves to ordinary folk, taking on forms such as cats, horses, or goats. They can also leave unsettling signs of their presence. For example, a cat boggart may leave paw prints on a clean kitchen floor or claw marks on the furniture.

Unlike other boggarts, stone chuckers cannot directly materialize, but when they want to scare people, they cover themselves in something visible, like mud or leaves, so that their true multiarmed shape can be seen. A terrifying sight indeed!

*Leys are lines of power beneath the earth: secret invisible roads that boggarts can travel. Several intersect underneath the Spook's Chipenden house, and sometimes you can hear a loud deep rumble as a boggart passes by below. This is particularly scary, and I've lost more nights of sleep because of this than I care to remember.—apprentice Paul Preston

All boggarts use ley lines* to travel from place to place, and when mobile they are called *free boggarts*. Sometimes disturbances to the leys, such as an earthquake hundreds of miles away, cause a boggart to become *naturally bound* and trapped in one location, unable to escape. Angered, this boggart immediately becomes very disruptive, and a spook may be required to drive it away.

All boggarts can understand human language, but most communicate with actions rather than words. If they are displeased, they show it by throwing and breaking things or being disruptive—for example, by digging up rows of potatoes after they have been planted, or opening gates to allow livestock to escape. If pleased, they may clean out a cowshed or wash and dry plates, placing them carefully back on the rack afterward.

Boggarts that talk, however, are difficult to deal with. Speech indicates a higher than usual intelligence. These creatures, combining this attribute with malicious behavior, are to be feared and dealt with very carefully indeed. It is usually necessary to slay them.

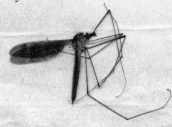

TYPES OF BOGGARTS

Bone Breakers

Bone breakers feed on the marrow in bones. Mostly they feast on dead animals, but they sometimes acquire a taste for the skeletons of recently buried people. This can be very upsetting for relatives of the deceased (and makes a lot of work for the poor sexton, who has to clear up the fragments of flesh and bone left behind in the graveyard). Worse still, bone breakers sometimes attack the living, wrenching bones from flesh while their victim is fully conscious. This is rare, but it does happen.

Henry Horrocks, the Spook who would, years later, become my own master, once had an apprentice killed by a bone breaker. I happened to pass by just

as Henry was about to bury the poor lad, who was lying by the graveside. I've never seen such a look of terror on a dead face. The boggart had really only wanted the thumb bone but had torn the lad's hand off at the wrist. He'd died of shock and loss of blood. It's a sight that I'll take with me to my own grave. The boggart was being controlled by a witch, who used it to gather thumb bones for her magic rituals. When two creatures of the dark cooperate like this, the danger is greatly increased. Even an experienced spook such as Henry can miscalculate—hence the demise of his poor apprentice.

Church Movers

These usually carry away the foundations of churches that are in the process of construction and place them elsewhere. There are many locations in the County— for example, at Leyland and Rochdale—where the new site chosen by the boggart has been accepted. The aim of the boggart is to remove the church from land where it has made its home, thus keeping people away. They rarely move the foundations of taverns, houses, or farm buildings, so it may be that, being creatures of the dark, the act of worship annoys them, causing a disturbance that they cannot tolerate.

Grave Wreckers

These boggarts smash tombstones, disinter corpses, and break coffins into tiny pieces. Like most of their kind, they feed on terror, but additionally draw extra strength from the outraged grief of the bereaved. They also collect bones, often hiding those they have stolen in deep caverns, where they are never seen again. Unlike bone breakers, they never feed on them, and as yet no spook has been able to discover why they do it and what purpose it serves.

Hairy Boggarts

These take on the shapes of animals such as black dogs, horses, goats, and cats. Goat boggarts and dog boggarts tend to be untrustworthy and malevolent. Cat and horse boggarts,* by contrast, can be friendly. They may even help with household and farmyard chores in exchange for being allowed to share a location undisturbed.

Very rarely, boggarts of this type can take *any* form they choose, usually in order to terrify their victim and

*I was born near Hackensall Hall and a glimpse of the horse boggart there, when I was just five years old, was my first warning that I had the gift of seeing the dead and other creatures such as boggarts. My father had left my mother, running off with another woman, and only years later did I learn that he had also been a seventh son. — apprentice James Fowler

grow stronger by feeding on that fear. I once had to deal with a boggart that took on the best-known shape of the Devil, complete with horns, tail, and cloven hooves. It could also talk, making it very dangerous indeed.

Hairy Boggart

Hall Knockers

Hall knockers frighten people by rapping on walls, banging doors, and generally causing a nuisance. If all your doors and windows are closed up tight when you go to bed, but you are still woken by slamming or rattling or loud noises in the night, then it's likely you are sharing your house with a hall knocker. They are very unpredictable and can be exceptionally dangerous. They may be stable for years, then change without warning into stone chuckers (see page 18).

One of the most notorious County hall knockers was located in Staumin. It caused severe disruptions in and around the church and manor house for many years. It was eventually bound by a priest. But he was no ordinary member of the clergy. A fully trained spook, who had taken holy orders afterward, he was one of my previous apprentices, Father Robert Stocks.*

* Father Stocks was killed in Read Hall near Pendle by the witch Wurmalde. He was a hard working and sincere priest and also a very capable spook who had for years kept the Pendle parish of Downham free of witches. — apprentice Tom Ward

15

Rippers

Without doubt the most dangerous category of all
boggarts is the ripper. These begin as cattle rippers,
which drink the blood of animals—usually cattle,
horses, sheep, or pigs. They can cause the farmer real
hardship by preventing his stock from thriving, but
eventually this type of boggart starts to kill, draining
its chosen animal slowly, visiting it many times until
the final encounter, when it drinks until the animal's
heart stops.

The very worst cattle rippers sometimes kill dozens
of animals in a single night. They rip open the poor
creatures' bellies or slit their throats, drinking only a
small amount of blood in each case. It is simply wanton

killing, done for the gruesome pleasure it affords the boggart. On such occasions, the howls of the boggart can be heard across the fields as it satisfies its blood lust. This is usually the final rogue stage, before the boggart becomes a full-blown ripper.

Rippers also drink the blood of humans, often trapping them in some way so they can't escape.* They will take small amounts of blood over several days but always finally gorge themselves so that the victim dies. Human blood has become a great delicacy for the boggart, something to be savored. After it has tasted human blood, it will kill and kill again until a spook is summoned to deal with it.

* I once had to try and save a priest who had been trapped by a ripper. It had split open the floor of a church and dragged the priest's leg into the crack, where it was slowly sipping his blood. Although I successfully freed the priest and bound the boggart—my first—the man died later because we had to amputate his leg in order to free him. —Tom Ward

The priest was my brother, and although we never got on well, his death saddened me greatly. Unfortunately he set in motion the chain of events by trying to rid himself of the boggart using bell, book and candle. Why do such people have to meddle? When threatened by the dark, it's sensible to send for a spook.
— John Gregory

Stone Chuckers

These boggarts throw pebbles, stones, or even boulders. Their intention is to terrify or slay those they wish to drive away from a chosen domain. Sometimes showers of stones rain down on a village or house for weeks at a time. These attacks are often fatal, making stone chuckers one of the most dangerous boggarts to deal with. An angry stone chucker is a terrifying sight to behold, with six huge arms, each hurling rocks. They need to be artificially bound or slain.

Whistlers

Feeding on fear, these boggarts attach themselves to anyone who appears susceptible. They whistle and howl down chimneys and through keyholes, using shrill, terrifying sounds as their weapon. Some victims are driven insane; others kill themselves. The wise ones send for a spook.

DEALING WITH UNKNOWN BOGGARTS

There are four stages when dealing with an unknown boggart, which may be easily remembered by use of the acronym NIBS (Negotiation, Intimidation, Binding, and Slaying).

STAGE 1: NEGOTIATION

The first step is to find out why a boggart is being troublesome and then make it an offer. This can simply be the respect of the people it is plaguing, or even their gratitude. It is, in fact, possible to live in the same house as a boggart and for the situation to be quite comfortable. Many boggarts respond to flattery. To illustrate this, I give below an account of my very first attempt to negotiate with a boggart.

THE CHIPENDEN BOGGART

After the death of my master, Henry Horrocks, I'd been plying my trade from the Chipenden house for less than a month when I was summoned to deal with a boggart. It had recently begun plaguing the workers at the local wood mill. A young spook must build his reputation carefully, and I was nervous at the prospect of having to prove myself so soon and so close to home.

Once all had left for the night, I wrapped myself in my

cloak and began my vigil in the large workshop with just a single candle to light the darkness. I expected to face a hall knocker because raps, bangs, and thuds had been disturbing the mill and frightening the workers who opened the premises in the morning and locked them at night. Tools and materials also seemed to have been moved and were found in unexpected places.

I'd salt in my right breeches pocket, iron in my left. When combined, they're the most effective weapon against a boggart, but I was ill at ease and not quite sure what to expect.

A hall knocker can become extremely violent, changing in the twinkling of an eye into a stone chucker. These boggarts can hurl boulders big enough to crush a man or pitch sharp shards of flint accurately enough to take out an eye, so I was ready for anything. But the first sounds I heard in the darkness told me that I was dealing with a hairy boggart.

I could hear the insistent *scritch-scratch* of sharp claws against wood, and as I watched, the boggart slowly began to materialize, taking on the shape of a large ginger tomcat.

I was both pleased and relieved, to say the least. Cat boggarts have a tendency to be benign and are more amenable to reason than their goat and dog counterparts. So I called out to it loudly but firmly, attempting to fill my voice with as much confidence as possible.

"Get you gone! Those who work here neither respect nor appreciate your worth. The ley is open, so move along! Choose a place where you'll be more comfortable! Find a location where you'll be welcome!"

No sooner had I spoken than the image of the large ginger cat faded and then disappeared altogether. For a few seconds, a loud purring filled the workshop, vibrating the floorboards and rattling the tools on the bench. Then all was silent. The boggart had gone! I was surprised at how easily it had yielded to my wishes.

It was with a sense of deep pride that I reported my success to the mill foreman the following morning. But as the proverb says, "Pride comes before a fall," and as I walked happily back to my house, already well paid for my services, little did I expect what was about to unfold.

As I lay in my bed the following night, I heard a tremendous tumult from the kitchen below—crashing and banging and clattering. It sounded as if all the plates in the kitchen were being systematically shattered and the pots and pans hurled violently against the walls.

Downstairs, my worst fears were proved correct. The kitchen was littered with broken crockery, and all the pans and cooking utensils had been scattered about the floor. To my dismay, it seemed that the boggart had taken my words as an invitation to move into my own house! As several ley lines pass under my Chipenden dwelling, it had managed this with ease.

I was really angry, and my first thought was to finish this malicious boggart off with salt and iron. But the wise teachings of my dead master prevailed. After all, the boggart was now in a fresh location, and the process of dealing with it should begin anew. It was only proper that I should try negotiation once more.

That night, in total darkness, I waited patiently in the kitchen for the hairy boggart to make its presence felt. Just before midnight, I heard a pan clatter across the stone floor.

"Why do that?" I asked in a calm and reasonable voice. "What have I done to hurt you? Why don't you just move on again and find somewhere more to your liking?"

A deep, throbbing growl of displeasure filled the darkness, making the hairs on the back of my neck rise and goose pimples stand up on my arms. I sensed that I was in the presence of a very powerful boggart, one that had just informed me, in no uncertain terms, that it had no intention of following my advice. Despite the fact that most cat boggarts are benign, on rare occasions some have shown themselves to be malevolent; a few are very dangerous indeed. If provoked, they can kill, delivering a blow hard enough to shatter a skull or tear out a throat with one swift slash of their sharp claws.

It was then that I had a sudden flash of inspiration. My master had told me that far to the south of the County, an old spook had once reached a comfortable accommodation with a boggart. In return for certain concessions, it had agreed to keep his house clean and tidy. So why didn't I attempt to do the same?

"Sounds like you don't much want to move on again. Well, I can tell you, I don't much want to move either, so we've reached a deadlock. We could fight it out until one of us is destroyed, but I think there's a better way to settle this. You and I need to come to an arrangement. Life could be very comfortable for both of us," I suggested. "Perhaps you could stay here and keep things tidy; also cook and clean for me. You'd never have to worry about being hunted and hounded by another spook, and on top of that I'd make sure you were well rewarded in other ways."

The boggart began to materialize again, taking the form of the large ginger tomcat. It glowed in the dark, and its fur was standing on end. Was it preparing to attack?

I thrust my hands into my pockets and pulled out two handfuls of what I'd stored there: salt in my right hand, iron filings in my left. The boggart saw my intention and let out a warning growl.

"Accept my offer or suffer the consequences!" I warned in reply.

For a moment we faced each other. Then the boggart slowly faded away. I waited in the darkness for almost an hour, just in case it returned. Finally I went off to bed, tired and worried. I felt I should have reacted faster and slayed the creature there and then.

But the following morning, there was a surprise waiting for me in the kitchen. A cozy fire was burning in the grate, and a hot meal was laid out on the table: bacon, eggs, and sausages, cooked to perfection. I ate with relish, but when I stood to leave the table, I heard a low angry growl. Thinking quickly, I realized my mistake and put it right immediately.

"My compliments to the cook," I said hastily. "That was just about the best breakfast I've ever tasted!"

At once there came a deep purring from beneath the table and I felt a big cat rub itself against my ankles. So far, so good. This boggart certainly appreciated flattery!

For a while things continued in the same way. Each morning an appetizing breakfast was waiting for me, and this was eventually extended to suppers as well. This continued—until, very gradually, things began to change and the quality of the cooking started to deteriorate. Some mornings the bacon would be burned or the eggs underdone. Then there came a time when no breakfast was waiting; that night, once again, I heard the sound of plates being smashed downstairs.

By the time I reached the kitchen door, the sounds had stopped, but I could hear the scritch-scratching of the boggart's sharp claws. I waited until there was silence, then, carrying a candle, finally entered that room. There, etched deeply into the wooden chopping block, were the words:

Well Rewarded?

Quickly I realized my folly. I had promised a reward but had failed to deliver. In that instant the candle blew out and the door slammed shut behind me. I was in grave danger.

I had salt and iron in my pockets, but this was a powerful boggart that had chosen not to show itself, so I had no means of locating my target. I reached for the door handle, and as I began to turn it, I felt a tremendous blow to my head that knocked it back hard against the frame. Befuddled and in pain, I stumbled to my knees. Then came the sharp sting of claws being raked down my right cheek. I was close to panic and scrambled to my feet, my heart racing with fear.

Somehow I managed to get the door open and stagger out of the room. There I looked in the mirror, examining the livid scratches on my face and listening to the smashing of crockery from the kitchen.

With the pain burning my right cheek, a lump the size of an egg on my head, and a raging headache, I had the whole night to consider my folly. I had, of course, promised a reward but allowed it to slip from my mind. Now the need to fulfill that promise was urgent. So I thought things through very carefully and by morning had an idea of how to proceed.

The following night I entered the kitchen with some trepidation and spoke to the invisible boggart.

"Your reward shall be my garden!" I called out. "In addition to cooking, washing, cleaning, and tidying, you will also guard the house and garden, keeping at bay all threats and dangers."

The boggart growled at that, angered that I'd demanded more work from it by extending its duties to the garden. Quickly I continued explaining what its reward would be.

"But in return for that, the garden shall also be your domain. With the exception of things bound within pits or chains, or my future apprentices, the blood of any creature found there after dark is yours to claim. But if the intruder is human, you must first give three warning howls. This is a pact between us, which will endure as long as this house has a roof!"

No sooner had I spoken than a deep purring commenced. The boggart was happy and the bargain was sealed. I immediately called at every house in the village and the neighboring farms, warning all that the garden was patrolled by a dangerous boggart and they would enter at their peril. Soon afterward I set up a bell at the withy-trees crossroads so that those in need of help could summon me rather than approach the house.

I have little fear that some innocent will ultimately fall victim to the boggart. Its warning growl can be heard for miles and is so loud and terrifying that any intruder would immediately flee. As for incursions by creatures of the dark, the boggart is strong enough to keep almost anything at bay.*

STAGE 2: INTIMIDATION

If negotiation fails, then an attempt should be made to intimidate the boggart by making its life in that location uncomfortable or even impossible. Salt and iron may be positioned strategically. Some boggarts take up residence in old thorn trees or store their power there. The tree may be chopped down or

---

* The boggart managed to keep the Priestown Bane at bay but it suffered badly and could have died. When it materialized afterward, it had been blinded in one eye.

We discovered another weakness of the boggart. It was tricked by a maenad assassin, who left blood dishes just outside the garden for the boggart to drink. There must have been something mixed into the blood because it didn't intercept the assassin; it only attacked and killed her when she was safely bound. The Spook considers it a real problem that might one day happen again. We are no longer as safe in that Chipenden house. —Tom Ward

burned, thus forcing the creature to search for a new location. Note that intimidation can often prove to be the most dangerous technique of the four. For, while a spook is annoying the boggart in an attempt to drive it away, the entity is unpredictable and may suddenly resort to extreme violence.

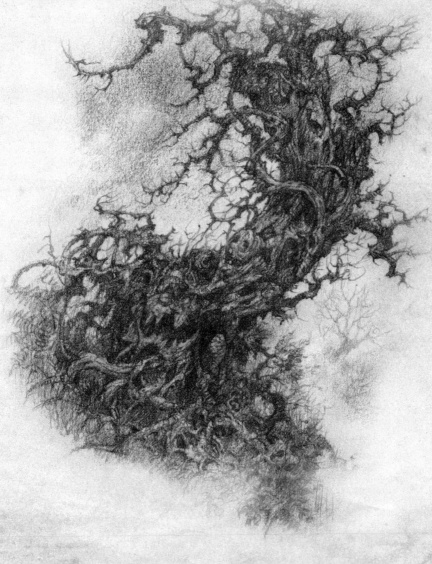

THE SAMLESBURY STONE CHUCKER

Toward the end of my first year at Chipenden I had to deal with a very dangerous boggart. It had made its home close to the village of Samlesbury, near the River Ribble, and in less than a month had transformed itself from a hall knocker, content to rap on doors and walls, to a fully fledged stone chucker, which was proving a real threat to the lives of the villagers.

For over a week stones had fallen on the village, breaking roof slates, chimney pots, and windows, terrorizing men, women, children, and animals. A stone chucker's objective is simple: It wishes to drive everyone away from land that it considers to be its own exclusive territory. When it claims ownership of a village and surrounding farmland, it must be relocated urgently.

My first task was to determine the location of its temporary home. This proved easy enough because, as usual, it was at the very center of the disruptions. On this occasion it had taken up residence in a cellar below the local tavern. I carried out the standard intimidation procedures, laying lines of salt and iron on the stairs, then mixing up a bone glue containing the same mixture and painting sections of the walls and doors with it.

That proved successful, and the howl as the boggart left its home could be heard for miles. However, I'd not anticipated its violent reaction. By way of reprisal, it killed the landlord of the tavern. That morning he was found in the yard under a very large boulder. Only his head, hands, and feet were visible. Once the boulder had been rolled away, we had to scrape the rest of him up from the flags. The boggart had turned rogue, a murderer of human beings, and now had to be slayed—a process I carried out to the letter.

I learned an important lesson from that unfortunate incident. Whenever I deal with a stone chucker, I now persuade everyone to leave the surrounding area until the job is completed successfully. Usually it just means finding a farmer and his family temporary accommodation, but if necessary I would evacuate a whole village.

STAGE 3: BINDING

To bind a boggart, a spook must first dig a pit and then coat the inside with salt and iron mixed into a bone glue. Next, a lid must be fashioned by a reliable stonemason, then hoisted into position directly above by a skilled rigger. To facilitate this, the mason attaches a hook to the top of the stone, which is later removed. After the underside of the stone has been coated with the mixture, a bait dish is filled with blood. This lures the boggart into the pit, at which point the stone is quickly lowered into position to bind it there.

Below are the important stages of the process.

1. Hire a master mason to cut and shape the stone lid
of the pit, and a rigger and his mate to lower that
stone safely into position. The tradesmen should
have previous experience of binding boggarts.
This is vital. Using inexperienced or unskilled
labor has cost the lives of both spooks and
apprentices.

2. Dig the pit, which needs to be at least six feet
deep and six feet square. This should be as close
as possible to the roots of a mature tree and
positioned beneath a branch from which the rigger

can hang a block and tackle. The oak is the best choice because such trees are the most efficient at slowly draining the strength of an imprisoned boggart, making it less likely to escape. (Note: The pit should be nine feet deep for a ripper.)

3. Mix the powdered cattle bone with water to make a thick glue. It is usual for the riggers to supply this and bring it to the location on their cart. When the mixture is sufficiently thick, add equal parts of iron filings and salt (half a standard sack in each case, also supplied by the riggers). Then stir thoroughly.

4. Using a block and tackle, and utilizing a strong branch, the rigger must now position the stone cover over the pit.

5. While this is being accomplished, use a brush to coat the inside of the pit with the glue mixture. This must be completed carefully, because to miss the tiniest spot would allow the boggart to escape.

6. Once the stone is suspended over the pit, its underside should also be thoroughly coated with the mixture.

7. Using a bait dish,* the boggart must be lured into the pit with milk or blood, the latter being preferable. (Blood is vital when dealing with a ripper.)

8. Once it has been lured into the pit, the rigger and his mate must quickly lower the stone lid into position. It is useful to have the mason also standing by to help with the positioning of the stone.

9. With the stone safely in place, the boggart is artificially bound.

BOGGART SIGNS

Spooks use a system of signs to mark the position of boggarts. This is both a warning to other spooks and a record of what has been done.

The sign above is typical of that found on the stone lid covering a boggart pit. The Greek letter beta indicates that a boggart is bound beneath the stone. The name (Gregory) tells who has carried out the binding. The rank 1 warns of the highest degree of danger (the ranks are graded from 1 to 10): a boggart of the first rank is very dangerous indeed and can kill without warning. The line sloping downward from right to left marks the boggart as having been artificially bound by a spook. More County spooks have died while attempting to bind boggarts than from any other cause. They are more prevalent here than anywhere else in the world.

A mark may be placed above the letter beta to signify the type of boggart bound—for example, the Greek letter P (rho) for ripper.

If the line slopes downward from left to right, the boggart is only naturally bound, probably as a result of some disturbance to the ley line that it has traveled to reach this place. In this case, the sign could be carved on a tree or scratched on a wall. A naturally bound boggart may break free at any time as a result of an earth tremor many miles distant.

THE FATES OF MY APPRENTICES

Being a spook is a dangerous business.* Some apprentices have been unlucky or just in the wrong place at the wrong time. Paul Preston, for example, was diligent and hard working; I had never seen a neater or more thorough notebook. All the preparation and knowledge in the world, however, would not have saved him.

* Two-thirds of my apprentices either failed or died while learning the trade. In addition to that, perhaps another ten fled into the night when taken to the haunted house at Horshaw to be tested. But only one of my apprentices turned to the dark. His name was Morgan, and he became a necromancer. He always sought an easy way to do things, and that was his downfall. Another weakness was laziness. He failed to apply himself properly to the study of the Old Tongue. — John Gregory

Paul was gored by a goat boggart as we crossed a muddy field near Wheeton. It intended to drive us away, but by mischance it achieved solidity the moment it made contact with my apprentice. Its horns entered just below his ribs, the left one spearing upward to pierce the heart. Poor unlucky Paul died instantly.

By contrast, some apprentices have brought misfortune upon themselves. I had taken to my bed with a severe fever and was forced to send my apprentice Billy Bradley out alone to bind a ripper, which is one of the most dangerous boggarts of all. I had trained the boy well and given him full instructions;

he should have been able to complete the task successfully. What went wrong must be noted so that no future apprentice ever repeats his mistakes.

Unfortunately, Billy was something of a daydreamer who never wrote up his notes with the thoroughness and detail required. To add to his lack of knowledge, there was a serious flaw in his character—that of impatience. The weather was bad, with wind and torrential rain, and Billy tried to complete the task too quickly. He lined the pit with salt and iron and managed to lower the bait dish in successfully, but he had already made one mistake that was to prove fatal.

Rather than hiring the very necessary experienced riggers, he had employed local laborers who lacked the necessary knowledge and skills. A block and tackle is the best device for positioning the stone; it uses a system of metal chains to lower the lid slowly and precisely. But you have to know what you're doing, and these men didn't. The stone trapped Billy's left hand, and before it could be released, the boggart bit his fingers off at the second knuckles and started to suck his blood. In the five minutes following this unfortunate incident, panic and sheer incompetence turned a retrievable situation into a tragedy.

The boy was screaming with pain, contributing to the terror and confusion. And whereas skilled riggers would have lifted the stone from Billy's hand in mere seconds, the hired laborers panicked. The stone was hoisted unevenly. The far side rose slightly and the chain jammed. The edge that had trapped Billy's hand pressed down on it even harder. By the time they managed to drag him free, the damage was done. The boy was unconscious and within moments stopped breathing. The shock and severe loss of blood had resulted in his death.

Billy had also made a second mistake. Being impatient, he'd failed to wait for the mason to return from his supper at a local tavern. Not only do masons cut and shape stone expertly; when working with riggers they are also skillful at positioning the lid of a boggart pit. The presence of the mason might just have saved Billy's life.*

STAGE 4: SLAYING

Finally, when all else fails, a boggart must be slain by casting salt and iron at it. It is important to get the timing right. Both substances must be hurled in such a way that they come together at exactly the same moment and envelop the boggart in a lethal cloud. Again, this takes a great deal of practice. Very powerful boggarts who can remain invisible even to spooks are particularly difficult to deal with.

* *Spooks and their apprentices are not permitted to be interred in church graveyards, so poor Billy was buried in unhallowed ground just outside the cemetery at Layton. He was my twenty-ninth apprentice. It is vital that lessons are listened to carefully, notes written up accurately, and instructions followed to the letter.* — *John Gregory*

They may be located only by the sounds they make and the direction from which objects are thrown. But as they get weaker and expend their energy, they gradually become visible. Stone chuckers are the worst of these to deal with.*

The method when dealing with a stone chucker is as follows:

1. Stir salt and iron into a bone glue.

2. If it is necessary to drive it away from human habitation, daub the mixture in all the places the boggart frequents. This stops it from taking refuge there.

3. Locate its true home. This is often a hollow tree. Stone chuckers prefer thorn trees.

* I encountered an extremely dangerous one at Stone Farm, near Owshaw Clough. After its thorn tree was chopped and burned down, the boggart relocated to Moor View Farm, to the west of Anglezarke Moor. I went out into the yard to present myself as a target for the stone chucker and so make it use up its power. It was a stormy night, and I needed the weakened boggart to enter the house, where the salt and iron would not be dispersed by the wind.

The boggart was very strong and battered me so hard that I almost died. I crawled back into the kitchen, using myself as bait so that it would follow. It was fortunate that my apprentice, Tom Ward, kept his nerve and slayed the boggart. It was many weeks before I made a full recovery.

Despite that, I did nothing wrong and dealt with the stone chucker according to the tried and tested method outlined here. Boggarts are dangerous creatures, and the risk of being maimed or killed goes with the job of being a spook. — John Gregory

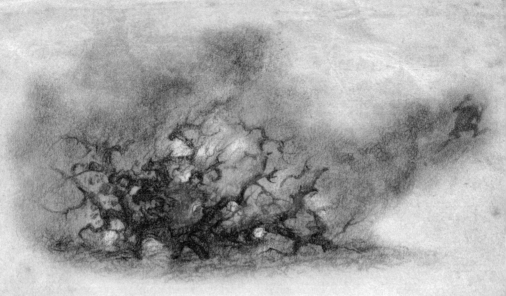

4. Chop down the tree and burn the roots. The creature has stored its power there, and by denying it that, you will make it less dangerous. Now angry and aggressive, it will seek out the one responsible for its woes.

5. Finally, present yourself as a target for the boggart. It will waste the last of its strength in trying to hurt you. It is best to do this outdoors, somewhere where there are few materials at hand. Even so, accept that you will suffer at least a few cuts and bruises.

6. When the boggart's strength is almost spent, lead it indoors, where the materials can't be dissipated by the wind. Use salt and iron to finish it off. Make sure to take aim with care. You will only get one chance!

Not all boggarts are as difficult to slay as a stone chucker. The secret is to be crafty and try to get close to your target.

THE COCKERHAM BOGGART

I arrived at Cockerham just after dark one evening, summoned there by the village schoolteacher, who met me at the churchyard gate.

"Thank goodness you got my message," he said. "You're only just in time."

Then he led me away from the church, down a narrow cobbled path between two overhanging buildings until we reached his cottage.

He was a typical village teacher, with bad dandruff and glasses with lenses so thick they gave him the appearance of a barn owl. He was also very tall and thin and bent forward from the waist. The wind could have blown him over at any moment—it was gusting hard, bending the branches of the sycamores and rattling the slates on the roofs. What caught my eye first, however, were his hands, which were large and bony, with long thin fingers. They were shaking so much that he had to try three times before he could insert his key into the lock. It was cold, but not that cold, so he was clearly terrified. Once inside, he offered me some potato soup, but I told him that I always fasted before spook's business.

"Tell me what your problem is," I demanded.

"There's not much to tell, but it's all bad," he said, his voice all of a quiver. "The Devil's here in Cockerham, and I've made a big mistake. I thought I was clever enough to deal with him, but I was wrong, and tonight at midnight he's coming back for my soul."

I smiled at him and, placing my hand on his shoulder, invited him to sit down. I tried to sound reassuring. "Why don't you start at the beginning and tell me the whole story?" I said. "Leave nothing out. Give me all the details. There may be something there that's important."

So the teacher began his tale. Most teachers like to talk, and enjoy the sound of their own voices; this one was different. Maybe it was because he was scared, but it took him less than five minutes from start to finish.

"The Devil's been visiting Cockerham every night for most of the winter," he said. "At first he just played tricks, rattling door knockers and overturning a few milk churns. But later he moved into the churchyard and started flattening gravestones, until finally he started frightening people to death—usually old people who live alone. Three have been found dead in just the past month, with such a look of terror on their faces that they've had to be put into their coffin facedown. Only then could the undertaker get up enough courage to nail down the lid.

"The villagers asked the parish priest to help, but after years of brave words in the pulpit, his response was disappointing. He suddenly decided to take early retirement, leaving the following day to live with his three sisters somewhere south of the River Ribble. So, having no one else to turn to, they finally asked me. They flattered me with kind words—told me I was the greatest scholar in the whole of the County; reminded me that I'd spent a lifetime reading and learning and passing on my knowledge to others. If anyone could get rid of the Devil, they said, it was me.

"Finally I agreed to help, not because of their flattery, but because I felt it was my duty. So, three nights ago, I cleared my schoolroom of all the desks but my own, and used my tattered and well-worn old copy of the Bible to summon the Devil.

"The malicious creature appeared immediately, threatening to drag me off to Hell, but then suddenly seemed to relent. With a sly look on his face, he ordered me to set him three tasks, promising that, if he was unable to complete just one of the tasks, he'd leave Cockerham immediately and never return. If he managed to do all three, however, my soul would belong to him for all eternity.

"I was so terrified I could hardly think and blurted out the first task that came into my head. 'Tell me how many grains of sand there are on Cockerham's shore,' I said. But immediately I realized my mistake. Cockerham's sands are very large and flat, but what are their exact boundaries? Is it the extent of the sands at the lowest tide or the highest? And where exactly do Cockerham's sands become Pilling's sands, the shore of the next village along the coast? But the worst problem of all was that I didn't know the answer to my own question.

"The Devil disappeared but was gone for less than three seconds. When he was standing before me again, he said a number so big that it was impossible to imagine. Too scared to challenge him, I could only accept his answer and set him another task. I was foolish for a second time. 'Tell me how many buds there are on all the sycamore trees in Cockerham,' I said. Again, it was a poor task because, whether the Devil really counted them or not, there was no way to check. I still didn't know the answer myself, so I just had to take his word for it. But finally I calmed down enough to ask for three days in which to think up a third task. The Devil agreed, and so I had just enough time to get word to you. Can you help me? I'm at my wits' end!"

"What did he look like, this Devil?" I asked.

"Just the way you'd expect, only worse," answered the teacher. "He had horns and a tail and he smelled like a goat. I've never felt so terrified in my life. That's why I couldn't think."

"Don't you worry," I reassured him. "I'll soon sort him out for you. Just take me to that schoolroom of yours and then come back here and heat up that soup for our suppers. Ten minutes after midnight, and it'll all be over."

There were just four things in the big schoolroom: the teacher's desk, a large cupboard, a sink with a tap, and the Bible, unopened on the desk. I'd taken off my cloak and hood because I didn't want to be recognized as a spook. I knew that the schoolmaster had really been plagued not by the Devil but by a dangerous hairy boggart that could talk and had the ability to shift its shape. As it had taken human lives already, I had no choice but to proceed to the fourth stage in the process, which was to slay it.

No sooner had I entered the room than there was a bright flash of lightning right outside the window, followed by a clap of thunder so loud that it made the roof shake and the floorboards vibrate beneath my feet. Distracted by that, I glanced toward the window. When I looked back again, something nasty was standing in front of the desk.

*Hairy Boggart
Disguised as
the Devil*

The boggart was exactly as the teacher had described, but no words could do justice to actually seeing it in the flesh. In addition to the curved horns and tail, it had cloven hooves just like a goat—and, yes, it certainly did smell very bad. Its body was covered in black hair that gleamed in the candlelight like the coat of a thoroughbred horse groomed for a big race. The face was very long, with two rows of brilliant white teeth.

But its tail reminded me of a rat's. It was long, thin, and black, and completely hairless. The boggart smiled at me then, a wicked, ugly smile that showed all its teeth. That long tail coiled and uncoiled, rapping three times upon the boards each time it was fully extended.

"What have we got here?" it asked, looking at me like I'd just been served up for supper.

"The schoolteacher's not feeling too well," I explained, "so he's sent me along in his place. I'm here to set the third task."

"Do you know the rules?"

I nodded.

"Good," said the evil creature, its tail rapping again on the wooden boards. "So get on with it. Set me my third task!"

"Weave a rope out of the best sand on Cockerham's shore," I said. "Then carry it back, wash it under that tap there, and give it to me."

I was pleased with the task I'd set, because even if the boggart did somehow manage to weave a rope out of sand, it would never be able to wash it under the tap because it would simply dissolve.

Witches can't cross rivers or streams, but all servants of the dark find running water extremely difficult to deal with.

The smile left the boggart's face. It frowned, showed its teeth, then disappeared. It was maybe all of five seconds before it stood before me once more, now holding a rope made out of sand but looking doubtfully toward the sink.

It didn't want to do it, but we had a contract of sorts and the creature had no choice. When it held the rope under the tap, of course, the sand just washed away between its fingers and ran down the plughole. So when the boggart walked back toward the desk, its face like a thundercloud, I gave a big smile in order to make it angry.

"I win," I said mockingly. "Off you go, right back to where you came from!"

It leaned across the desk toward me until its forehead was almost touching mine, and the mean, vindictive expression on its face told me that it had no intention of keeping its end of the bargain. The boggart's breath smelled so bad that I moved back a little, but not too far. Just so that I could reach into my breeches pockets.

I hurled something white from my right hand and something dark from my left. Salt and iron. Salt to burn the boggart; iron to bleed away its power. They came together, a lethal-white-and black cloud, just as they struck the creature's face and shoulders.

What happened next wasn't a pretty sight. The boggart, howling fit to wake the dead, began to crumple and melt. Within seconds it was nothing more than an unpleasant puddle on the schoolroom floor.

After that I went back and had supper with the schoolteacher, explaining that we'd been dealing with a boggart rather than the Devil. He listened patiently, but I'm not sure he really believed me. Later he must have told his version of what happened to all who'd listen, explaining how he'd cleverly invented a third task that the Devil couldn't perform.

Years later, the tale of how a clever Cockerham schoolmaster outwitted the Devil is still being told across the County. To make things worse, he never did pay me for getting rid of the boggart!

NOTORIOUS BOGGARTS

NAME:	Bury Boggart
CATEGORY:	Bone breaker—used by the witch Anne Caxton to snatch the bones of the living for dark magic
RANK:	1
BOUND OR SLAIN:	Slain
SPOOK:	Henry Horrocks (my own master)
APPRENTICE IN ATTENDANCE:	I was with Horrocks but didn't become his apprentice until five years later
NUMBER OF VICTIMS:	Three, including his former apprentice, Brian Harwood

NAME:	Coniston Ripper
CATEGORY:	Cattle ripper turned rogue
RANK:	1
BOUND OR SLAIN:	Slain
SPOOK:	Bill Arkwright
APPRENTICE IN ATTENDANCE:	None
NUMBER OF VICTIMS:	Thirty at least

NAME: *Wheeton Goat*
CATEGORY: *Hairy boggart*
RANK: *2*
BOUND OR SLAIN: *Slain*
SPOOK: *John Gregory*
APPRENTICE
IN ATTENDANCE: *Paul Preston*
NUMBER OF VICTIMS: *One—my apprentice, Paul Preston*

NAME: *Horshaw Boggart*
CATEGORY: *Cattle ripper turned rogue*
RANK: *1*
BOUND OR SLAIN: *Bound*
SPOOK: *Thomas Ward (apprentice)*
NUMBER OF VICTIMS: *One—my foolish priest brother*

NAME: *Pendle Ripper*
CATEGORY: *Cattle ripper turned rogue; used by Malkin witch clan to attack their enemies*
RANK: *1*
BOUND OR SLAIN: *Still at large*
NUMBER OF VICTIMS: *More than one hundred deaths in forty years*
CURRENT SITUATION: *Active more than seventy years ago, now dormant; controlled by dark magic*

NAME: *Layton Ripper*

CATEGORY: *Cattle ripper turned rogue*

RANK: *1*

BOUND OR SLAIN: *Slain*

SPOOK: *John Gregory*

NUMBER OF VICTIMS: *Just one—my apprentice Billy Bradley, who behaved rashly*

NAME: *Rivington Sheep Ripper*

CATEGORY: *Cattle ripper turned rogue; got a taste for shepherds*

RANK: *1*

BOUND OR SLAIN: *Slain*

SPOOK: *John Gregory*

NUMBER OF VICTIMS: *Six; killed five shepherds and a parish constable*

NAME: *Staumin Hall Knocker*

CATEGORY: *Hall knocker*

RANK: *1*

BOUND OR SLAIN: *Bound*

SPOOK: *Robert Stocks—by then he had a second trade at his fingertips: He was also a priest*

APPRENTICE
IN ATTENDANCE: *None*

NUMBER OF VICTIMS: *One suicide induced by fear*

The Bane

THE OLD GODS

One common debate among spooks concerns the true nature of the Old Gods. There are those who believe that they are not all denizens of the dark and that some are actually benign.

It is true that some seem more evil and cruel than others, but to me the case is beyond dispute. The Old Gods trifled with human emotions, behaved selfishly, caused wars and inflicted terrible cruelties on humankind. Many demanded blood sacrifices. They are all creatures of the dark.

Aphrodite

Her name is derived from the Greek word *aphros*, which means foam. She was said to have been born from the ocean waves, already a fully formed adult. The golden daughter of Zeus, she presides over all things beautiful in the world. However, she has a malevolent destructive side and seems to delight in the power her beauty allows her to wield over men.

Aphrodite also has the power to drive away storms and calm the winds. Some say she is the wife of

Hephaestus, the blacksmith of the gods. It is strange that the ugliest of the Old Gods should win for his bride one of the most beautiful. Or perhaps she used her allure to bind him to her in order to gain some as yet unknown advantage.

Artemis/Hecate

Another goddess who originated in Greece, Artemis is a cruel huntress, a lover of woods and wild places.

Hecate

Beautiful and athletic, she draws the admiration of all men but also takes on a different, hideous shape—that of Hecate, sometimes called the Queen of the Witches. She rules over gloomy places and is especially to be feared on the darkest of nights, when there is no moon.

She is also said to linger near crossroads, taking the souls of those who pass by. Although supposed to be the protector of the young, she sometimes demands blood sacrifices, and many maidens have been put to death in order to placate her. Hecate is another dangerous female to beware of.

The Bane

The Bane was originally one of the Old Gods, worshipped by an ancient people called the Segantii (sometimes also called the Little People). He lived in the long barrows at Heysham but was free to roam the whole County.

The Bane's physical form was hideous, his squat, muscular body vaguely human in shape but covered in scales, with long, sharp talons sprouting from fingers and toes. His face was ugly indeed, with a long chin that curved upward almost as far as his nose and large ears that resembled those of a wolf.

The Bane terrorized everybody, including the king of the Segantii, King Heys. The Bane demanded a yearly tribute, and King Heys was even forced to sacrifice his own sons. One son died each year, starting with the eldest, but the last and seventh son, Naze, managed to bind the Bane.

He died in doing so, but the Bane was now trapped in the catacombs under Priestown Cathedral behind a silver gate, his strength diminished so that he was no longer a god. The only way he could ever get free was for someone to open that gate.

Over time, despite his imprisonment and initially weakened state, the Bane slowly grew in power.

The Bane

Eventually, whisperings could be heard in some of the cellars of the houses facing the cathedral. These voices gradually became deeper and more disturbing, and the floors and walls would shake and vibrate under the influence of the Bane's rumbling bass voice.

In recent times the Bane has grown even more powerful and is trying to regain the physical form he possessed so long ago. He can also shift his shape, read minds, and even look out through the eyes of others. Slowly he is starting to control the priests in the cathedral above the catacombs. A great danger now lies in wait for anyone who goes down into the catacombs: the press. The Bane can exert a tremendous pressure, crush bones, and smear the unfortunate victim into the cobbles that line the tunnels.

He has a few weaknesses, however. He needs blood, and will take that of animals if humans aren't available. But humans must give their blood freely— though when faced with the terror of the press, most will do so eventually. If he has to make do with rats and mice, the Bane grows weaker. He can also be hurt by silver—especially a silver blade. Women make him nervous, and he will often flee from their presence.* Hence his victims are usually male.

*It is certainly true that females make the Bane nervous. In the labyrinth beneath Priestown Cathedral, Alice drove the Bane away by hissing and spitting into its face. —Tom Ward

MY FIRST ATTEMPT TO DEAL WITH THE BANE

When I was in my prime, five years after first becoming a spook, I attempted to deal with the Bane. Although bound behind the silver gate under Priestown Cathedral, he was slowly growing in power and needed to be slain.

I entered the town under cover of darkness and went directly to the shop of my brother, Andrew, who was a master locksmith. He feared that I would not survive an encounter with the Bane, but reluctantly agreed to fashion me a key to the silver gate.

We set off for an abandoned house very close to the cathedral; one haunted by a powerful strangler ghost. It was enough to deter people from living there and I'd not tried to send it to the light, because its presence guaranteed that I would always have that access to the catacombs. I'd been planning this attempt on the Bane for over two years.

By means of a trapdoor in the cellar, we climbed down into the crooked cobbled tunnels and headed in the direction of the silver gate. Once there, Andrew drew in a deep breath to steady his shaking hands and took a wax impression of the lock.

Back in his workshop, he shaped the key while I slept: I needed to rest after my journey and gather strength for the struggle ahead. By dusk the key was in my hands, and I set off alone through the dark and deserted streets of Priestown. Using the trapdoor of the haunted house once more, I was soon down in the tunnels. When I reached the gate this time, my own hands began to tremble. Would the key work? Even if it did, there was great danger in opening the gate. The Bane might be lying in wait close by and seize his chance to escape.

One thing reassured me, though. The Bane lacked the power to know what was going on in every corner of the labyrinth, and the instincts of a seventh son of a seventh son were very useful. I closed my eyes and concentrated. Instinctively I felt that the Bane was not nearby, so I inserted the key into the lock. Andrew had done a good job: It turned easily, and the gate swung open. Wasting no time, I closed and locked it again.

So that I wouldn't get lost in the labyrinth, I used the same method that Theseus employed to kill the minotaur and escape from a similar maze. I carried with me a large ball of twine and tied one end of it to the hinges of the silver gate. That done, I set off into the darkness, slowly unraveling the twine. In my right hand I carried my staff and candle; my silver chain was tied about my waist; salt and iron were in my pockets. Thus prepared, I began an exploration of the tunnels.

I hadn't been walking along the tunnels for much more than half an hour when a cold feeling ran down my spine, the warning that something from the dark was very near. I halted, placed the candle on the floor, and pressed the recess on my staff so that the blade emerged with a click. Then I untied my silver chain and coiled it about my left wrist, ready to throw. I waited, my heart hammering in my chest, trying to control my breathing.

I would get but one chance. Only if the Bane materialized, taking on a definite physical shape, would I have some hope of dealing with him. A spook cannot usually hope to triumph over one of the Old Gods, but his confinement in the labyrinth meant that he was now no more powerful than a demon; that was bad enough, but he did have weaknesses. So I felt certain that my silver chain could bind him—for a while. That would give me time to drive my silver-alloy blade through his heart, and I hoped that would finish him off forever. At least I had to try.

But in his spirit form I had no defense against it. None whatsoever. I hoped that he would just see me as another victim, easy prey. When he attacked, I would be ready.

There was a deep growl from the darkness where the tunnel curved away to the left and the Bane padded into view. He had taken on the shape of a large black dog with sharp yellow teeth and powerful jaws. Saliva dripped from his mouth to splatter on the cobbles; he was hungry for my blood but, unlike a ripper boggart, could not take it unless I gave it freely. It used terror and pain to persuade his victims. First he would seize me in his jaws.

He loped forward, then sprang straight toward me. I unfurled my silver chain and cast it at my assailant. It cracked and dropped toward the head and shoulders of the Bane, but then the beast twisted in midair and the edge of the chain just caught his shoulder. I heard him scream at that contact with silver, but then he simply vanished.

Despite hurting my enemy, I knew I was defeated as good as dead. My only chance of victory had been to pierce his heart with my blade. Now he was in his spirit form, and I had no defense against him. He would never leave the labyrinth. He would now use the press against me, exerting its power until I was crushed and smeared into the cobbles. But he spoke first. I thought he did so partly to torment me, partly to fill me with terror so that I would give my blood freely. But it wasn't my blood he wanted. It was freedom!

"I'm got proper in this place!" his voice moaned to me out of the darkness. "Bound fast, I am. But you came through the gates and must have a key. Open it for me! Let me out and I'll let you live!"

"Nay! I can't do that!" I replied. "My duty is to the County. I must keep you bound within these tunnels even at the price of my own life."

"One more time I'll ask. Set me free or I'll make an end to you!"

"Make an end to me now. Get it over with because my answer's still the same."

"Get it over with?" growled the Bane. "Not so easy as that. Take my time, I will, and press you slowly. . . ."

With those words, my staff was dashed from my hand and an invisible weight fell onto my shoulders and forced me to my knees. The pressure was steady at first and not unbearable, but the creature was toying with me, and much worse was to come. I was pushed backward, and within a few minutes lay on my back on the cobbles. The weight pressing me down became so great that I couldn't move a muscle and was struggling to draw breath.

Some cruel quisitors test suspected witches by placing thirteen heavy stones, one by one, on the woman's supine body. The weights are calculated carefully so as to inflict the maximum torment. Only as the eleventh stone is placed upon her chest does it become almost impossible to breathe. The placing of the thirteenth stone usually results in death as the organs are crushed and there is internal bleeding. Now I was being subjected to a similar process, except that instead of stones, the Bane himself was exerting an invisible pressure. But just when I was about to lose consciousness, thinking my end had come, the press would ease and I would awake to more torment.

"One more chance! One more chance I'll give you! Will you set me free?"

By then I was unable to speak but just managed to give a slight shake of my head.

"So now I'll make a end of you!" cried the Bane.

This time the pressure on my body increased rapidly, and

within moments I was no longer able to breathe. My eyes grew
dim, and I could taste blood in my mouth. I was beginning to
resign myself to death when something happened that I had never
experienced before.

I heard a scream of fear and pain, and suddenly the weight
was gone from my body. The Bane had fled—I felt sure of it. But
why? I was too weak to turn my head, but out of the corner of
my right eye I could see what looked like a column of light. It
was the form that a ghost sometimes takes—though the color was
wrong. Ghosts are a pale white; this was a strong, shimmering
purple. And from it waves of warmth and peace seemed to radiate.
I closed my eyes and, completely unafraid, slipped down into a
darkness that could have been death.

I was unconscious for days and woke up in the guest bedroom
above Andrew's shop. Concerned that I'd not returned from the
catacombs, Andrew had crafted another key and, managing to
overcome his terror of the Bane, had gone through the silver gate
to find and retrieve me.

I was in a bad way, with five broken ribs and bruises all over
my body, so I recovered only very slowly. Even now I don't know
what drove off the Bane and saved my life. Perhaps it was some
sort of spirit from the light, ensuring that I survived. *But why?* I
wonder.

Could it be that I have something of importance to do
beyond the routine tasks of a County spook? I don't believe in
the God that priests preach about in their churches. Not for me,

a grim old man with a white beard. But that wasn't the only time I've been helped in a time of need. Often I've felt that something was standing at my side, lending me strength. I have come to believe that when we face the dark, we are never truly alone.

The Fiend

The Fiend is the dark made flesh, the most powerful of all its denizens and the very oldest of the Old Gods. He has many other names, including the Devil, Satan, Lucifer and the Father of Lies. It is believed that he meddled in the affairs of humanity from the earliest times, gradually growing in power as the dark strengthened. At some point he walked the earth in a reign of terror lasting over a hundred years but then returned to the dark. Occasionally he passes through a portal and visits our world—usually at the instigation of a witch or mage who seeks power through satanic magic. The most famous pact between a human and the Fiend is that of Faustus (see page 67), but there are many others, some barely remembered now.

The Fiend sometimes makes a special bargain with a witch.* In exchange for bearing him a child, her power is increased. He hopes that the child will be an abhuman, witch, or mage and will grow up to serve

* Last year, the Pendle witch clans united, the three covens performing a ritual to bring the Fiend through the portal and allow him to stay in our world indefinitely. They only controlled him for two days; now he is his own master and poses the biggest threat to the County since the records in my library began. His influence upon our world is waxing, along with that of the dark. Churches lose their congregations, war grows more savage, and men forget their humanity; father is turned against son, marriages fail, and famine and disease increase. — John Gregory

The Fiend

the dark. There is one other benefit of such a liaison to a witch: once the Fiend has visited her child, he can no longer approach the mother for as long as she lives, unless she wishes it. Henceforth she is free from his influence and meddling.

The Fiend has many supernatural powers. He can make himself large or small, taking on any form he desires, either to trick or terrify people.* His true shape is said to be so terrible that one glance can drive people insane or cause them to die of fright. He can appear out of thin air, look over a victim's shoulder, and even read human minds. Often he remains invisible, but his cloven hoofprints can be seen burned into the ground. He can also manipulate time—speeding it up, slowing it down, or even halting its flow entirely.

Above all, he is crafty and treacherous. Rather than resorting to force, he often uses trickery and deceit.

*The Fiend took on the shape of bargeman Matthew Gilbert, who was murdered by the water witch Morwena. It was impossible to tell that it wasn't the bargeman: In appearance and voice they were identical. - Tom Ward

SATANIC MAGIC

This magic is earned at great cost by making obeisance to the Fiend, often known as the Devil. Such worship is fraught with danger, as the worshipper, mage, or witch gradually grows less human and more subservient, eventually becoming merely a tool of the dark.

The highest and most dangerous form of satanic magic is obtained in return for selling one's soul to the

Devil. However, he is usually sly and subtle, getting the best part of the bargain—as can be seen from the following account.

THE FAUSTIAN PACT

Faustus, the foremost scholar of his age, was disappointed by the limited knowledge available to him. He had mastered the main university subjects but found that they neither provided answers to the big questions he asked nor granted him the power he sought.

He fell into bad company, and a dark mage lent him a grimoire—a book of magic containing a spell to raise the Devil or his servants. After dithering for many days, Faustus finally used the spell to summon an assistant to the Devil, a lesser devil called Mephisto. On behalf of his master, Mephisto made a pact with Faustus. In return for knowledge and power, the scholar agreed to surrender his soul at midnight twenty-four years after the bargain was made. Faustus signed the contract in his own blood. He attempted to do this three times—on the first two occasions, the blood dried too quickly for him to write his name. It is said that this was angels of the light attempting to save his soul. But finally the pact was made, and Faustus was doomed.

Using satanic magic, Faustus became the most notorious mage in the known world, visiting the courts of kings and emperors to display his magical power: levitating, making himself disappear, or conjuring wonders from thin air. But as time went on, Faustus began to realize that he'd been cheated. He could not create life or learn all the secrets of the universe. These things were denied to him because the Devil did not have the power to supply them. They belonged to the light and were beyond the reach of dark magic.

There were times when Faustus longed to repent, but each time the Devil appeared to the mage in his true shape and terrified him so much that he was forced to continue with his wicked ways. Finally the twenty-four years approached their end, and at midnight the Devil was due to come for Faustus's soul.

He tried to pray; tried one last time to turn back to the light. It was no use. Years of bad habits were ingrained in his soul, and he failed. In the next room, three scholars from the university prayed for his soul, but their prayers went unanswered. At midnight they heard terrible noises from Faustus's chamber: thuds, bangs, terrible tearing sounds, and then, loudest of all, the screams of Faustus. Then all became ominously silent.

They waited until daybreak to enter. The floor was wet with blood. The body of Faustus had been torn to pieces by the Devil, and his soul dragged off to the domain of darkness.

No one should ever make a pact with the Fiend. For its practitioners, satanic magic is the most dangerous category of all.

Golgoth

Golgoth is also known as the Lord of Winter and was worshipped so fervently by the first race of mankind that he was able to pass through a portal from the dark to dwell on earth for thousands of years. He has the power to create local pockets of cold so extreme that human flesh and bone become brittle and can shatter into fragments. It is believed that Golgoth caused at least one of the great ages of ice.

Golgoth now sleeps* under a large barrow on Anglezarke Moor, known as the Round Loaf because of its shape. For the sake of the County and the world beyond, let us hope that he continues to do so.

*Twice in my lifetime Golgoth has awakened; both events were facilitated by a human agency— that of my former apprentice, Morgan, who used a grimoire.
—John Gregory

Golgoth

Hephaestus

Hephaestus* was the blacksmith of the Old Gods; he fashioned tools and weapons to serve their interests during the first age when they all dwelt in this world. At that time humans had yet to emerge from their caves, where they cowered in fear of the terrible external forces that might extinguish all their lives. Hephaestus was the only one of the gods considered to be ugly. Some say he was also lame. He has fallen silent and now sleeps in the dark, but he has left a dangerous legacy.

* Although my second eldest brother received the name James in the local church, my mam's secret name for him was Hephaestus. How apt that he should grow up to follow the trade of a blacksmith! Another example of Mam's ability to see into the future. —Tom Ward

Hephaestus

There are supposedly weapons still in existence that were manufactured by Hephaestus. The most famous, a sword able to cut through any armor and even stone, is said to make its bearer invincible. It is also reputed to be a potent weapon against demons and other denizens of the dark. The king who last owned it was betrayed, his sword stolen, and he was slain. People say that it was sealed in an ancient barrow* with the king's body, somewhere to the south of the County, but the precise location is unknown.

Another weapon forged by Hephaestus, which has also left Greece, is a war hammer that never misses its target and always returns to its owner's hand. It is believed to be in the possession of one of the strigoi, the vampiric demons that dwell in Romania (see page 187).

*Barrows are interesting and mysterious. Most probably contain more than just the bones of the dead: some surely hide powerful artifacts.— apprentice Morgan Hurst

The Morrigan

This is the female Old God who is worshipped by the Celtic witches in that mysterious place called Ireland, which lies over the sea far to the west of the County. We cannot be sure of the extent of her powers, but she is also known as the goddess of slaughter.

When a witch summons her to our world, she may take the shape of a large black crow and alight on the left shoulder of one who is soon to die. Additionally,

The Morrigan

she sometimes scratches the heads of her enemies with her claws, marking them for death. In this shape the Morrigan frequents battlefields, pecking out and eating the eyes of the dead and wounded.*

The Ordeen

This female deity is the most powerful agent of the dark in Greece. She visits our world every seven years. While most other deities who use portals need the help of humans, the Ordeen does not.

* When we faced the banshee witch, the Morrigan, in the shape of a crow, attacked Bill Arkwright, scratching his head with her claws. He was killed by fire elementals within one year of that attack. —Tom Ward

The Ordeen

Little else is known about her other than she is extremely bloodthirsty.* Her chief worshippers are maenads, but she brings other denizens of the dark through the portal with her, particularly flying lamias, demons, and fire elementals. Between them they slaughter all in their path, and the bloodshed spreads for many miles around. Few survive to record what happens during these visitations, so knowledge is limited. It's a mercy that the County is apparently beyond her reach.

Her maenad supporters usually confine themselves to their homeland, Greece, and draw their power from a mixture of wine and blood. Under its influence they fly into a frenzy and fight their enemies with a wild fury. Sometimes they use blades, but they are phenomenally strong and can dismember enemies with their bare hands. They are slowly regressing, emotion taking over from intellect, and it is likely that they will eventually lose the power of speech and, like water witches, become more animal than human.

---

* I saw the Ordeen at close quarters, and she was truly terrifying. Initially she had the form of a human female but with a rank animal smell. Her teeth appeared very sharp and her jaws powerful. But after I bound her with my silver chain, she took on her true shape — that of a huge lizard with green scales, a salamander. She spat fire and scalding steam at me, and when I tried to slay her with my staff, it burst into flames and turned into hot ash in seconds. —Tom Ward

Although they worship the Ordeen, gathering in great numbers to await her arrival, they receive no reward for their services; after she and her followers have ravaged the land, they feast upon the blood of the dead and the dying.

The maenads have scryers but do not use mirrors. After forcing quantities of wine down the throat of a sacrificial goat, they slit open its belly and study its intestines. By such means they claim they can peer into the future.*

* Since the above entry, the Ordeen has been destroyed. As I was one of the group who brought this about, I am in a good position to record what we learned. The portal used by the Ordeen to come into this world was both breathtaking and terrifying—a pillar of fire extending from earth to sky. Through it came an immense citadel known as the Ord, many times the size of Priestown Cathedral. Within it were many traps and dangers, not the least being a multitude of fire elementals, including both translucent and opaque orbs, and also asteri.

It was the first time I'd ever seen fire elementals, but they behaved as other spooks have recorded, and this enabled me to fight them off, so we owe a great debt to the past. On the roof of the main structure were a large number of abhuman spirits, no doubt trapped by the Ord over aeons as it passed backward and forward through the portal.

What is truly worrying, though the threat from the Ordeen now seems to have ended, is that we did not discover how she could visit our world without human intervention. If that ability were shared by another of the Old Gods, such as Golgoth or Pan, life on earth would become even more difficult and dangerous. —John Gregory

Pan (the Horned God)

Pan is the Old God, originally worshipped by the Greeks, who rules over nature and takes on two distinct physical forms. In one manifestation he is a boy and plays a set of reed pipes, his melodies so powerful that no birdsong can equal them and the very rocks move under their influence.

Pan

In his other form he is the terrifying deity of nature whose approach fills humans with terror—the word "panic" is derived from his name. Now his sphere of influence has widened and he is worshipped by the goat mages of Ireland (see page 148). After eight days of human sacrifice, Pan passes through a portal from the dark and briefly enters the body of a goat. He distorts the shape of that animal into a thing awful to behold and drives the mages to perform more and more terrible acts of bloodshed.

Portals

These are magical doorways through which the Old Gods can pass to enter our world.* Human intervention is usually required to make this possible, but there are four particular locations where portals may occur. These are also places where elemental spirits evolve naturally and can become sentient and powerful.

The first is the County in England, where witches have always attempted to communicate with servants of the dark, particularly the Fiend. And within the

---

* I have now seen three of the Old Gods enter our world through portals. The first was Golgoth, when Morgan used a pentacle to conjure him into our world. The second was the Ordeen, who entered via her own fiery portal. The third, and perhaps the strangest, was when the banshee witch summoned the Morrigan to kill me, using her own mouth as the portal. — Bill Arkwright

County itself, the prime place for portals is the Pendle district, where the brooding presence of the hill aids all types of dark magic.

The second is Greece, where mages and witches have communicated with the dark from ancient times, probably before such activity was observed in the County. This is the land where the Ordeen rules; she is the only one of the Old Gods who can emerge through a portal without human aid.

Thirdly, there is a district of Romania called Transylvania, known as the Land Beyond the Forest, where vampiric creatures are legion and the most powerful of the Old Gods, Siscoi (see below), rules the mountains and forests. Aided by witches, he frequently passes through a portal, but even from the dark he can possess both the living and the dead.

Fourthly, in the southwest of Ireland is a mysterious region where goat mages and Celtic witches dwell. The former worship the Old God Pan; the latter worship the Morrigan, the goddess of slaughter (see page 71).

Siscoi

This powerful vampire god is frequently brought through a portal into the Romanian province of Transylvania. He is the lord of the numerous vampiric creatures that dwell in the mountains and forests of that remote region. Even from his abode in the dark, and without making use of a portal, he can send out his spirit to reanimate the dead or possess the living.

Romanian spooks have many successful methods for dealing with ordinary vampires, but they are utterly powerless against Siscoi. He is now the most active and malignant of the Old Gods, even surpassing the Ordeen in ferocity.

Siscoi sometimes animates the skin of a newly buried corpse: His minions first remove the bones and skillfully rend the skin from the muscle; the latter they devour. The reanimated corpse appears to the close relatives of the dead. Siscoi appears before his victims as the bloated skin of their loved one, filled only with air. But as he begins to feed, the corpse skin fills up with blood, turning red in the process.

Zeus

Zeus was once the leader of the Old Gods, sometimes given the title King of the Gods. Like his subjects, he once walked the earth but has not passed through a portal from the dark for many thousands of years. He is no longer worshipped widely in Greece, and his power has lessened.

Lord of the storm, controller of the sky, his preferred weapon was the thunderbolt, using lightning to incinerate his enemies. Zeus had many relationships with mortal women, who gave birth to his children. His jealous wife, Hera, punished those she discovered, among them Lamia (see page 96).

Zeus

A Pendle Witch

WITCHES

Witches have walked the earth from the earliest times, and the development of human language has allowed them to weave ever more complex curses, spells, and rituals. By trial and error they have also learned the potential of plants to either poison or cure. Some witches are benign healers, following a path toward the light and helping their communities; others choose to ally themselves with the dark, lured to sell their souls in exchange for the ability to wield dark magic.

HOW TO TEST A WITCH

Throughout time, witches have been seen as rivals to organized religion, and consequently persecuted. Some have been burned, some hanged, others drowned or decapitated. Certain tests are used to decide whether or not a woman is a witch. These are usually administered by a witchfinder or quisitor, an agent of the Church, although some communities take the law into their own hands. Many of these tests do not work, and spooks don't hold with them.*

*Testing a witch? Just never trust a woman. And never trust a woman who wears pointy shoes. — John Gregory

* The principle behind the swimming test is right — it's just the practice that is wrong. Most witches cannot cross running water, so a stream or river would be a better place to test them. Witches also find seawater toxic because of its high salt content. — Bill Arkwright

Swimming has been the test most frequently used. The suspected witch is taken to the nearest pond or lake and her hands tied to her feet before she is thrown in. If she floats, she is presumed guilty and taken away to be burned. Sinking supposedly proves her innocence, but in sinking, many innocent women drown or die of pneumonia or shock. Swimming someone in a lake or pond does not work as a means to identify a witch; whether the woman floats or not depends on luck and the kind of body she has.*

Pricking is equally cruel. A pin or bodkin (a sharp dagger) is jabbed hard into the flesh of a suspected witch in order to find the devil's mark. The object is to discover a section of her body that cannot feel pain. Sometimes the mark is invisible, but a mole or skin discoloration is considered strong evidence of the guilt of the accused. Again, this is not a sufficient test for finding a true witch.

Pressing involves using thirteen stones. The witch is tied down onto a wooden rack, and the stones are then laid on her body one at a time. Once all are in place, she is left for an hour before the stones are removed. If she survives, it is assumed that the Devil has saved her and she is hanged. Some quisitors use stones so heavy that the suspected woman is pressed to death—either her internal organs are crushed, or she suffocates.

85

Alternatively, in some parts of the world quisitors use the stones as a means to force a confession from a suspected witch. After the eleventh stone, she is barely able to breathe, but one nod will free her from the press. Yet in admitting that she is a witch, the unfortunate woman has signed her own death warrant.

Human Witches

Water witches and lamia witches are only partly human, but each fully human type of witch can be divided up into four general categories.

The Benign

These are wise women who have a great knowledge of herbs and potions. Some are midwives, others healers, and they have saved countless lives. They serve the light, and any monetary gain is small. If their clients are poor, they will usually work for nothing.

In the County there are a number of benign witches, mainly healers and midwives. The foremost among them are:

Maddy Hermside of Kirkham
Jenny Bentham of Oakenclough
Eliza Brinscall of Sabden
Angela Nateby of Belmont
Emma Hoole of Rochdale
Madge Claughton of Samlesbury *

*These women can be relied on to help spooks and their apprentices with their local knowledge and healing capabilities. Charges of witchcraft may be brought against them from time to time, and we should be prepared to defend them and educate their neighbors where necessary.

*Agnes Sowerbutts of Pendle could fall into the category of a benign witch, but her status is not certain. She is a healer but uses a mirror for magical purposes, something usually considered a tool of the dark. —Tom Ward

THE FALSELY ACCUSED

These are poor women wrongly persecuted by a witchfinder. Often they are victims of malicious gossip, but sometimes conspiracy is involved when the witchfinder colludes with neighbors in order to have an innocent woman tried and condemned, usually with a view to seizing her house and possessions.

THE MALEVOLENT

These witches draw power from the dark and pursue their own ends—either without any consideration of the consequences for others, or deliberately setting out to do harm. While some serve the Fiend directly, many act of their own volition. There is also a whole spectrum of power and ability. At the lowest end of the scale, witchcraft is dabbled in to survive; it is a means to fill the belly and gain shelter against the cold ravages of winter. Such witches are little more than beggars. At the highest end of the scale, whole kingdoms may rise or fall at the whim of a powerful witch.

THE BINDING OF MOTHER MALKIN

The most dangerous malevolent witch I ever had to deal with was, without doubt, Mother Malkin. She had a long history of slaying children. Living on boggy moss land, far to the west of the County, she had once offered homes to young women who, although expecting babies, had no husband to support them. For this supposedly charitable enterprise, she earned the title Mother. It was, however, a cruel ruse: Years later, when the local villagers finally grew suspicious and drove her out, they found a field full of bones and rotting flesh. She had slain both mothers and babies to feed her insatiable need for blood.

Mother Malkin

I'd spent the long cold winter at my house in Anglezarke, returning late in the spring to find that Chipenden had been terrorized in my absence. Mother Malkin wasn't working alone; she was with her son, a terrifying creature known as Tusk, and her granddaughter, Bony Lizzie. During that long winter people had been afraid to venture out after dark, and the threesome had used the time to steal, intimidate, and commit murder.

Five local children had been taken, the last over a month earlier so there was no hope of retrieving them alive; they would have been sacrificed for blood magic. All I could do was prevent further abductions by dealing with the witches and their thuggish accomplice.

Tracking them down wasn't difficult, as they had set up home in an abandoned farm about three miles southeast of my

Tusk

Chipenden house. As I was dealing with three adversaries, I was
forced to compromise: I had only one silver chain and could
therefore only hope to bind one witch and put her in the pit
I had already prepared in my eastern garden. But I also hoped
to drive off the other two and make the area safe once more.
First I decided to dispose of the creature. It was clear why the
villagers had nicknamed him Tusk. His canine teeth were huge
and horribly deformed, protruding sharply from his mouth.
He was dangerous and immensely strong, so my first priority
was to prevent him from getting too close to me. Many of the
victims that were dug up from that boggy moss land had clearly
suffered broken ribs. It was thought that Tusk had squeezed the
breath from their bodies, shattering their bones in the process.
I waited until he returned one night, his large sack of ill-gotten
gains over his shoulder, and followed him back through the trees.

"Put that down, thief!" I called, putting a mixture of disdain and imperiousness into my voice in an attempt to rile the creature so he would charge me recklessly.

It worked almost too well! Even faster than I'd anticipated, he whirled round, dropped the sack, and charged straight at me, bellowing like an angry bull. I used my staff, stepping to one side to deliver a heavy blow to his head. He went down hard but scrambled back to his feet within seconds to attack once more. Four or maybe five times I managed to fend him off, bringing him to the ground on two occasions at least. But he became wilder and more aggressive, and I began to tire. I was worried that he'd succeed in grappling with me at close quarters. I had two witches still to deal with, so it was time to finish it.

I pressed the recess in my staff, and with a click, the retractable blade emerged. I was prepared to kill him—after all, he'd already played his part in the abduction and murder of children. When he charged again, I wounded him in the shoulder. Even that was not enough to deter him, so the next time I stabbed him in the knee. He fell down in the long grass and howled with pain like a whipped dog. He started to crawl away from me, so I let him go. He was no longer a threat, and my priority was the witches.

I set off for the house of Mother Malkin and Bony Lizzie. As expected, they'd sniffed out the danger and were waiting for me in the trees as I approached. They were strong and very malevolent. The old one, Mother Malkin, used dark magic against me—the powerful spell called dread. I'd never experienced anything like it, and waves of fear washed toward me so that I began to shiver, shake, and sweat. For a few moments I couldn't move; I stood there, struggling even to breathe, while the younger witch, Bony Lizzie, slowly moved closer, her eyes glistening with blood lust, a sharp blade raised to take my life.

My perceptions distorted by the spell, I saw the two women as demons with horned heads and the forked tongues of fanged snakes. Only by a great effort of will was I able to swing my staff and dash the blade from Lizzie's hand. That done, I stunned her with a blow to the head and turned my attention to Mother Malkin. She was by far the more dangerous of the two, the one I most needed to bind.

Mother Malkin and Bony Lizzie

I reached under my cloak and eased my silver chain onto my wrist. As I approached, she began to back away warily. Casting a silver chain is a skill that must be honed, and I've always practiced dutifully, routinely throwing the chain at a post in my garden. Of course, it's far harder to cast successfully against a moving target, and other factors have to be allowed for, such as the force of the wind and the elevation of the ground.

I cracked the chain and threw it, and it fell in a perfect spiral to enfold the witch and tighten against her limbs and teeth. She collapsed into the long grass, twitching and struggling, but to no avail. Seizing her by the left foot, I dragged her for quite some distance until she became quiet. Once she was docile, I carried her over one shoulder back to my eastern garden, calling in at the outskirts of the village on my way to hire the services of the local stonemason and blacksmith.

Under my supervision, they fashioned a stone border for the pit I'd already prepared, and the witch was safely bound. I was pleased with how things had turned out—but that night, to my surprise, the other witch made an approach to the garden in a hopeless attempt to rescue Mother Malkin. The roar uttered by the boggart must have made her almost jump out of her skin. She ran, but I gave chase. Her flight was difficult because there are many streams east of Chipenden and a witch cannot cross running water! There were no witch dams here, such as one found in the Pendle district.* Nonetheless, she had a good head start and I was unlikely to catch her. Instead I shouted out to her,

* Witches (with the exception of water witches) cannot cross running water. As the Pendle district has numerous streams, some means had to be found to enable witches to move about relatively freely. Thus witch dams were developed. A system of pulleys and a handle are used to lower a big wooden board into a stream to block its flow. The heavy board slides down between two grooved posts into a trench in the bottom of the stream, which is lined with wood to make a good seal. Water quickly builds and flows around the dam, but before it does so, several witches are able to cross safely. —John Gregory

telling her of the terrible fate that awaited her should she dare to return. And when she turned to check my progress, I whirled my silver chain aloft to drive the point home.

After that I was content to let her go. The warning from the boggart and the fate of Mother Malkin should have scared her badly, making it unlikely that she would venture into the area of Chipenden again.*

The following day I searched for Tusk; on further reflection I had decided to take his life. There were bloodstains in the grass and a clear trail where he had crawled away, but the signs ended mysteriously; clearly, powerful dark magic was involved. Despite my best endeavors I was unable to track him down.†

* Now I know better. Time has shown that I was wrong to allow Bony Lizzie to escape, and I also should have killed Tusk while I had the chance. Years later, both returned to Chipenden in another attempt to free Mother Malkin. It almost cost me the life of my apprentice, Tom Ward. (How we finally dealt with Mother Malkin is chronicled in Tom Ward's own notebooks.) I have always had a tendency to be merciful. Sometimes it has cost both me and others dearly. — John Gregory

† From what has been learned since the return of the Fiend to this world, it is highly probable that Tusk was an abhuman, the result of a union between a witch and the Fiend. — John Gregory

The Unaware

It is possible for a witch to live out her whole life and not once realize her potential. This never happens in witch communities such as Pendle: here, an unaware witch is quickly sniffed out by the coven and pressure put on her to develop her abilities for the good of the clan. But in some isolated villages, the ability may jump two or three generations and suddenly manifest itself in a child who is completely unaware of her own power. Sometimes this is revealed in a crisis: For example, when her own life or that of a loved one is threatened, a witch's latent power may flare up. Even then, many attribute it to a "miracle" or the intervention of some deity, rather than realizing that the true power lies within.

Celtic Witches

These witches come mainly from the southwestern regions of Ireland, sometimes known as the Emerald Isle because of its lush green grasslands, a consequence of even heavier rainfall than the County endures. It is a mysterious land, often shrouded in mist.

Little is known about these Celtic witches other than they worship the Old God called the Morrigan (see page 71) and operate alone (they do not belong to clans). They also form temporary alliances with the goat mages of that region, who sometimes use them as assassins to kill their enemies.

Lamia Witches

The first Lamia was a powerful enchantress of great beauty. She loved Zeus, the leader of the Old Gods, who was already married to the goddess Hera. Unwisely, Lamia then bore Zeus children. On discovering this, the jealous Hera slayed all but one of these unfortunate infants. Driven insane by grief, Lamia began to kill children wherever she found them, so that streams and rivers ran red with their blood and the air trembled with the cries of distraught parents. At last the gods punished her by shifting her shape so that her lower body became sinuous and scaled like that of a serpent.

Thus changed, she now turned her attentions to young men. She would call to them from a forest glade, only her beautiful head and shoulders visible above the undergrowth. Once she had lured her victim close, she wrapped her lower body around him tightly, squeezing the breath from his helpless body as her mouth fastened upon his neck until the very last drop of blood was drained.

Lamia later had a lover called Chaemog, a spider thing that dwelled in the deepest caverns of the earth. She bore him triplets, all female, and these were the first lamia witches. On their thirteenth birthday, they quarreled with their mother and, after a terrible fight, tore off her limbs and ripped her body to pieces. They fed every bit of her, including her heart, to a herd of wild boars.

Chaemog

The three lamia witches reached adulthood and became feared throughout the land. They were long-lived creatures and, by the process of parthenogenesis (needing no father), each gave birth to several children. Over centuries the race of lamia witches began to evolve and breeding patterns changed. Those who consorted with men took on human characteristics and sometimes bore hybrids; those who shunned human companionship retained their original forms and continued to give birth to fatherless children.

Lamia witches can now be classified as either feral or domestic. The former retain the shape of the originals—the triplets who emerged from Lamia's womb. In their feral form, the majority scuttle about on all fours, have sharp claws, and drink the blood of humans and animals. They use blood magic and can summon victims to their presence and hold them in thrall just as a stoat transfixes a rabbit. Their homeland is Greece, but they often range far beyond that nation's boundaries and have been found in the County.

Those classified as domestic are human in appearance, but for a line of green and yellow scales that runs the length of the spine. They also use blood magic but augment this with bone magic; some even use familiars (see Witch Powers, page 120).

Lamia witches are slow shape shifters. Those who associate with humans gradually take on the human female form. The opposite is also true. Bound in a pit, or somehow cut off from communication with humans, a domestic lamia witch gradually reverts to her feral form.

A Feral Lamia

Some feral lamias, called vaengir,* also have wings and can fly short distances, attacking victims from the air. These are relatively rare and seem doomed to extinction.

Hybrid lamias take many forms. Those born of human fathers are never totally human or totally lamia.

* Inside the Ord there were hundreds of vaengir summoned by the Fiend to swell the ranks of the Ordeen's servants. This accounts for them rarely being seen elsewhere. — Tom Ward

Á Vængir

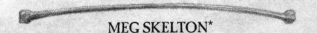

MEG SKELTON*

One of the natural enemies of a spook is a witch, so it pains me to confess that the love of my life was the witch Meg Skelton. As a young man, I rescued her from a tower where she had been imprisoned by an abhuman who had been terrorizing the district, a fierce creature that I slew with my staff.

Finding Meg bound with a silver chain, I released her, and such was her powerful allure that I fell in love with her there and then. But when the morning came, I saw the line of green and yellow scales running the length of her spine and knew that Meg was a lamia witch in her domestic form, and that it was my duty to bind her in a pit. I dragged her to its edge, but finally could not bring myself to do it. Love binds a man tighter than a silver chain.

We walked away hand in hand and lived together for one happy month in my Chipenden house. Unfortunately Meg was strong willed, and despite my advice she insisted on visiting the village shops. Her tongue was as sharp as a barber's razor, and she argued with some of the village women. A few of these disputes developed into feuds. No doubt there was spite on both sides, but eventually, being a witch, Meg resorted to witchcraft.

She did no serious harm to her enemies. One was afflicted by nasty boils all over her body; one exceptionally house-proud woman suffered recurrent infestations of lice and a plague of cockroaches in her kitchen. At first the accusations were little

*This is the account of my dealings with the lamia witch Meg Skelton. She has now returned to her homeland, Greece, and I do not expect to see her again. I include it now as a warning to my apprentices.
—John Gregory

more than whispers. Then one woman spat at Meg in the street and received a good slap for her discourtesy. It would have stopped at that, but unfortunately the woman was the sister of the parish constable.

One morning the bell rang at the withy-trees crossroads and I went down to investigate. Instead of the poor haunted farmer that I expected, the stout, red-faced parish constable was standing there, truncheon in his belt and hands on his hips.

"Mr. Gregory," he said, his manner proud and pompous—had I been a poor farm laborer, the weapon would already have been in his hand—"it has come to my attention that you are harboring a witch. The woman, known as Margery Skelton, has used witchcraft to hurt some good women of this parish. She has also been seen at midnight, under a full moon, gathering herbs and dancing naked by the pond at the edge of Homeslack Farm. I have come to arrest her and demand that you bring her to this spot immediately!"

While Meg always gathered herbs at the new moon and did indeed dance naked, she had the power to ensure that, unless she wished it, nobody could see her. So I knew that the last of the charges was a lie.

"Meg no longer lives with me!" I said. "She's gone to Sunderland Point to sail for her homeland, Greece."

It was a lie, of course, but what could I do? There was no way I was going to deliver Meg into his hands. The man would take her north to Caster, where no doubt she'd eventually hang.

I could see that the parish constable wasn't satisfied, but there was little he could do. Being a local, he dared not enter my garden for fear of the boggart, so he went away, his tail between his legs. I had to keep Meg away from the village from that day forth. It proved difficult and was the cause of many arguments between us, but there was worse to come.

At the insistence of his sister, the constable went to Caster and made a formal complaint to the high sheriff there. Consequently they sent a young constable with a warrant to arrest Meg. I was concerned for his life—he was an outsider and might be stubborn enough to enter my garden. I'd been warned about this by the village blacksmith, so I was ready. With the smith's help I managed to persuade him that Meg really had left the shores of the County forever.

Disaster had narrowly been avoided—but that decided me. My former master, Henry Horrocks, had left me another house on the edge of brooding Anglezarke Moor. I had visited it just once and found little about it to my taste. Now it could be put to good use. In the dead of night, very late in the autumn, Meg and I journeyed to Anglezarke and set up home there.

It was a bleak place, wet and windy, with the winter threatening long months of ice and snow. Even though I lit fires in every room, the house itself was cold and damp—not a place where I could safely store books. We made the best of it for a while, but eventually the same problem reared its head when Meg insisted on doing the shopping.

I managed to persuade her to avoid Blackrod, a village where I had family, but she started to have problems in Adlington.

It began in a similar fashion to the difficulties in Chipenden. A few words were exchanged with the local women: accusations of using curses; a woman suffering night terrors; another too afraid to venture beyond her own front door. This time the local constable didn't get involved because the people of Adlington had a strong sense of community and believed in sorting things out for themselves.

I told Meg not to visit Adlington again and employed the village carpenter, a man called Shanks, to bring groceries up to the house. She was angry at that and we quarreled bitterly. After this, there was a coldness between us to rival that of the winter on Anglezarke Moor. It persisted, and three days later, despite my protests, Meg went shopping again.

This time the village women resorted to violence. Over a dozen of them seized her in the market square. Shanks told me that she'd fought with her fists like a man but also scratched like a cat, almost blinding the ringleader of the women. Finally they struck her down from behind with a cobblestone; once felled, she was bound tightly with ropes.

Only a silver chain can hold a witch for long, but they rushed her down to the pond and threw her into the deep, cold water. If she drowned, they would accept that she was innocent of witchcraft; if she floated, they'd burn her.

Meg did float, but facedown, and after five minutes or so

became very still in the water. The women were satisfied that she had drowned, so they left her where she was.

It was Shanks who pulled her out of the pond. By rights she should have been dead, but Meg was exceptionally strong. To Shanks's amazement, she soon began to twitch and splutter, coughing up water onto the muddy bank. He brought her back to my house across the back of his pony. She looked a sorry sight, but within hours she was fully recovered and soon started to plot her revenge.

I'd already thought long and hard about what needed to be done. I could cast her out—let her take her own chances in the world. But that would have broken my heart because I still loved her.

My knowledge of a special herb tea seemed to be the answer. It is possible to administer this to keep a witch in a deep sleep for many months. If the dose is reduced, she can be kept awake but docile: She can walk and talk but the tea impairs the memory, making her forget her knowledge of the dark arts. So this was the method I decided to use.

It was very difficult to get the dosage right, and painful to see Meg walking about so subdued and mild, her fiery spirit (something that had attracted me to her in the first place) now dampened. So much so that she often seemed a stranger to me. The worst time of all was when I left her alone in my Anglezarke house and returned to Chipenden for the summer. It had to be done, lest the law catch up with her. There was still the danger of her being hanged at Caster. So I locked her in a dark room off the cellar steps in so deep a trance that she was hardly breathing.

I left for Chipenden with a heavy heart. Although I'd experimented through the winter, I still worried about whether or not I'd gotten the dose right. Too much herb tea, and Meg might stop breathing; too little, and she could wake up alone in that dark cell with many long weeks to wait until my return. So I spent our enforced separation riddled with sorrow and anxiety.

Fortunately I had calculated the dose correctly and returned late the following autumn just as Meg was beginning to stir. It was hard for her, but at least she wasn't hanged, or exiled to Greece. The County was spared the harm she could inflict.

But a lesson must be learned from this, one that my apprentices should note carefully. A spook should never become romantically involved with a witch; it compromises his position and draws him dangerously close to the dark. I have fallen short in my duty to the County more than once, but my relationship with Meg Skelton was my greatest failing of all.

Water Witches

These witches are far more animal than human and have mostly lost the power of speech. They dwell in marshes, rivers, canals, and ditches, and, unlike human witches, have the ability to cross running water.* However, they cannot use mirrors, either to communicate or to spy on others. One name commonly given to water witches is greenteeth, because of the green slime that sometimes forms on their lips and teeth. Children are often warned by their parents to

---

* Seawater, with its high levels of salt, is toxic for witches. They avoid the seashore and cannot safely walk on sand even when the tide is at its lowest ebb. Even water witches die if immersed in seawater for too long. However, witches can and do make successful sea voyages. To do so, they must stay in the boat's hold as much as possible and dress to shield their skin from the wind and spray.
—John Gregory

Bill Arkwright uses a salt solution in the pits he uses to bind water witches. This makes them docile. He also has a salt moat around his garden to keep others at bay.—apprentice Graham Cain

A Greentooth

keep away from all places where greenteeth might be lying in wait.

Their noses are sharp and without flesh, while their canines are elongated into immense fangs. They hook their prey using razor-sharp taloned forefingers. Sometimes they strike into the cheek or ear, but their aim is to pierce the upper neck and wrap a finger around the teeth, taking a firm grip upon the jaw. That grip is almost impossible to escape from, as water witches are extremely strong. They drag their victims into marsh or water and drain them of blood as they drown.

MORWENA

The oldest and most powerful of all the water witches
is Morwena. She may be more than a thousand years
old, and her father is the Fiend, her mother a witch
who dwelt in the deepest and dankest
caverns of the earth.

In addition to the attributes
of a common water witch
(with even greater speed
and strength), she has a
blood-filled eye with
which she is able to
paralyze her victims.
There are limitations
to her power, however:
That eye can only be
used against one person at
a time. She must also conserve
its strength, and when she isn't using it,
she pins her top and bottom eyelids together over
it with a piece of sharp bone. A further weakness
is that, even more than other witches of her type, she
may not stray too far away from her element—bog
and water—or her strength begins to wane.

For the definitive account of this water witch, refer
to Bill Arkwright's book, *Morwena*.

Morwena

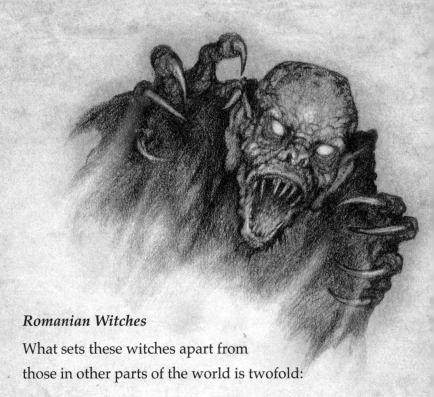

Romanian Witches

What sets these witches apart from
those in other parts of the world is twofold:

1. The ability to project their souls far from their
   bodies while they sleep. These meet up with other
   souls in forest dells, taking the form of small orbs
   of flickering light that move together rhythmically
   in a dance. These disembodied covens are not
   always thirteen strong, which is usual elsewhere,
   but they are always odd in number, most
   frequently dancing in sevens, nines, or elevens.
2. If humans see the moving lights, they are drawn
   toward them and are soon in thrall to the witches.
   When the dance ends, the humans die, the witches
   having gradually absorbed their vitality.

Romanian witches use animism magic (see page 120); which means that rather than using blood or bone magic they draw out the life essence of their victims and use it, along with rituals and incantations, to gather power from the dark.

They worship Siscoi, the Romanian Old God, and have the power to bring him through a portal into our world at midnight—though he can stay only until dawn. They also form alliances with strigoi and strigoica, vampire demons, and can control Transylvanian elementals known as the moroi as an aid to draining humans of their life force.

The dark magical power gained is used primarily for the following:

1. To summon their vampire god, Siscoi, from the dark.
2. To kill their enemies.
3. To scry the future.
4. To control the humans who live within their chosen domain.
5. To gather wealth.

Romanian witches are very rich and live alone in big, isolated dwellings. They do not form clans, and the only time they meet is when they send forth their souls to combine temporarily in covens.

WITCH GROUPINGS

Clans

A witch clan is composed of family groups. Not all members of such a clan will necessarily be witches, but they will support those who are.

The three main clans in Pendle are the Malkins, the Deanes, and the Mouldheels. Witches often migrate to places that are a source of power or have the right ambience for performing dark magic. It was the brooding presence of Pendle itself that drew the clans to that area.

First came the Malkins, who now operate from their stronghold, Malkin Tower. They are not only the oldest, but also the most powerful clan. The original tower was owned by a local landowner called Benjamin Wright. He was a strong, stubborn man, and it took the witches three years to drive him out, using curses, poison, and finally the abduction of his eldest son. Once Benjamin Wright vacated the tower, his son was released. Unfortunately it happened too late: The boy was already insane and died within the year.

From then the building became known as Malkin Tower. The witches extended it—mainly downward, where deep dungeons and an escape tunnel were excavated. The mortar that binds the stones of the tower is brown because it is mixed with human blood and powdered bone. Usually only the Malkin coven and a few supporters live in the tower. Most of the Malkins reside in the village of Goldshaw Booth.

The Deanes were the second group to migrate to Pendle. Their families came by boat from Ireland, the wet, misty land across the western sea.

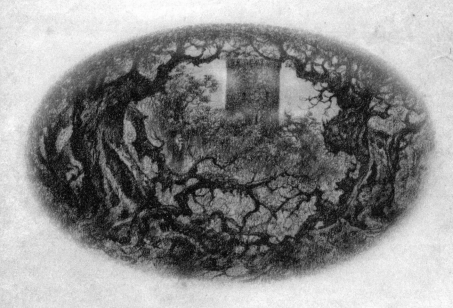

Malkin Tower

Bloodthirsty battles were fought against the Malkins in Crow Wood, but they failed to capture Malkin Tower. So they made their home in the village of Roughlee. The Deanes are the proudest of the main clans and are easily insulted. Sometimes they imagine grievances and become spiteful and vindictive. They still dream of making Malkin Tower their own. Although Celtic in origin, after centuries of life in the County they gradually changed their ways. Their families interbred, formed the Deane clan, and ceased worshipping the Morrigan.

The Mouldheels, formerly nomadic, were the last of the main clans to arrive. These witches went barefooted, and behind their backs, some called them "stink feet" or "moldy heels," the latter evolving into their present name. The village of Bareleigh eventually became their home.*

The three main witch villages lie quite close together in an area sometimes known as the Devil's Triangle. There are other Pendle witch clans, but these are smaller and much less powerful. Among them are the Hewitts, Ogdens, Nutters, and the Preesalls.

---

* The current leader of the Mouldheels is Mab. She's a very young but powerful witch and an extremely skilled scryer. Beware—she will use fascination against a spook if she can! —Tom Ward

There are also some more recent incomer witches, although these are shunned.*

Covens

A coven means thirteen witches gathered to use dark magic, usually at celebratory feasts such as Candlemas (February 2), Walpurgis Night (April 30), Lammas (August 1) and Halloween (October 31).

The covens gather at midnight on those feasts, and occasionally, drawing strength from the adulation of his worshippers, the Fiend materializes briefly to accept obeisance and grant dark power.†

Witch Assassins

Each Pendle witch clan (most notably the Malkin, Deane, and Mouldheel families) employs at least one witch assassin—whose primary role is to seek out

* *The powerful witch Wurmalde journeyed from Greece to Pendle and succeeded in briefly uniting the three main clans to bring the Fiend through a portal to this world. That witch is dead now, and the clans are in conflict once more. We must be watchful lest another outsider comes to bring the Malkins, Deanes, and Mouldheels together again.—John Gregory*

† *These former appearances of the Fiend often lasted just a minute or so. Now, of course, he dwells in our world and threatens it with a new age of darkness.—John Gregory*

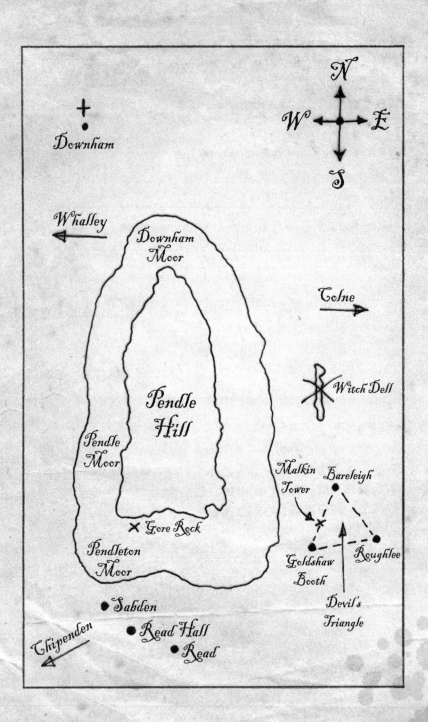

and destroy their enemies. The successor is usually chosen by a challenge followed by mortal combat. The Malkins' assassin is easily the most formidable. Three challengers are trained each year and take turns fighting her.

The current assassin of the Malkin clan is Grimalkin. Very fast and strong, she has a code of honor and never resorts to trickery. She prefers her opponent to be a real test. Although honorable, Grimalkin also has a dark side and is reputed to use torture.

All fear the *snip-snip* of her terrible scissors. She uses these to shear the flesh and bone of her enemies. She carves this sign on trees to mark her territory or warn others away. Grimalkin's favorite killing tool is the long blade, and she is a skilled blacksmith who forges her own weapons.

Grimalkin

OTHER NOTABLE MALKIN WITCH ASSASSINS

The previous Malkin assassin was Kernolde the Strangler, who, in addition to blades, used ropes, traps, and pits full of spikes to capture and slay her enemies. Once victorious, Kernolde habitually hung her victims by their thumbs before slowly asphyxiating them. She always faced challengers in the Witch Dell, north of the Devil's Triangle. There she was aided by the dead witches who haunt that place, particularly Gertrude the Grim, who has been dead for over a century. Kernolde was finally slain by Grimalkin, who hung her by her feet so that the birds could peck her bones clean.

The assassin known as Needle used a long spear as her primary weapon. She impaled her victims and watched them die slowly. After losing an eye to a poisoned dart, she went into decline, finally being defeated in combat by Kernolde.

Dretch was one of the very first Malkin assassins, and the clan still talks of her to this day. She could stalk her enemies with such skill that it was impossible to hear her approach. Her primary weapons were her fingernails and her teeth. In combat, she would blind her enemy with her nails and bite savagely into the throat, tearing out an artery. She was ambushed by a dozen Deanes on Walpurgis Night, when there is traditionally a truce between the clans. After a fierce fight she was slain, but five of her attackers paid with their own lives. This began a year-long war between the Malkins and the Deanes.

Demdike was the only assassin ever to have been murdered by her own clan—the Mouldheels. She made powerful enemies by disobeying directives and insulting the Mouldheel clan leader to her face. At the Halloween sabbath they took her by surprise, stoned her, and threw her body into the fire.

Kernolde

WITCH POWERS

Animism Magic

This type of magic is also practiced by the category of mages known as shamans, but its strongest adherents are the Romanian witches. They feed upon the animus, the life essence of a creature. This is not its soul; it is the vitality or energy that animates body and mind. They do not take blood but draw the animus forth directly by use of willpower and incantations, sometimes over many weeks or months. The body of the victim becomes gray and wrinkled and withers until the skin is like dry parchment over the brittle bones. Sometimes, in the later stages, the victim appears dead but still walks. He breathes and his heart beats feebly, but his eyes are unseeing and he cannot speak. At that stage, death is very close.

Very occasionally, when seven or more witches are gathered together, the victim drops dead within seconds. Again, the feeding is accompanied by exertion of the group willpower and incantations. Romanian witches never write down any of their spells; they are passed through the generations and learned by heart.

Blood Magic

This is the most basic of the types of magic practiced by witches. They may progress to the higher levels of bone magic or familiar magic, but all start at this stage and continue to use it from time to time throughout their lives.

Blood features in rituals, especially at the time of the four main witches' sabbaths (February, April, August, and October). Drinking copious amounts, especially the blood of children, increases the potency of dark magic. It enhances both scrying and cursing, the latter being used to bring about the death of an enemy from a great distance.

Bone Magic

This type of magic is one level higher than blood magic. The bones of animals can be used, but human bones, especially thumb bones, are the most valued. The thumb bones of a seventh son of a seventh son are the greatest prize of all.*

Using bones in rituals can achieve a variety of things. One of the most notorious uses is to create a bone yard, a deadly place to trap the unwary. After drinking blood squeezed from the thumbs of a still-living victim, the witch invokes the dark, using incantations, then cuts away the thumb bones and buries them at the center of the yard.

* The witch Bony Lizzie had me trapped in a pit and was ready to take my bones. She was already sharpening her knives when Alice helped me escape.
—Tom Ward

When someone wanders into the boneyard, their own bones become very heavy and they are bound to the spot; slow starvation is the result. At the center of

such a trap, the pressure exerted is so great that the victim's bones are broken and crushed. To reach that point is rare, however; it is a fate usually suffered by an animal such as a hare or deer that is moving very fast. Once the flesh has rotted and fallen away, the witch comes to claim her harvest.

When approaching the lair of a bone witch, always move with extreme caution. The first warning when entering a boneyard is a feeling of lethargy, soon followed by a sense that your whole body is becoming heavier. But it is important not to panic. To turn around can alert the witches that a victim is trying to escape and causes the pressure to intensify. So start to move backward very slowly, taking deep breaths. Once clear, find another route to the witch's lair, but beware of further traps.

Witches can also use bone magic to enslave graveside lingerers, ghosts bound to the scene of a crime or confused spirits wandering in limbo.* Once a spirit is summoned, a witch enslaves it and can make it do her bidding, often using it to spy on or terrorize enemies.

Sometimes bones are ground down to a fine powder and mixed with blood before being sipped from a human skull. Not only does this provide an easy way to get bone into the witch's body, it adds an element of blood magic as well, thus heightening the power of the ritual.

Curses

In conjunction with blood or bone magic, witches routinely use curses to kill their enemies from afar.[†]

---

* Limbo comes from the Latin word limbus, which means the edge or fringe. Souls have to pass through it to reach the light. Some find it harder than others. — John Gregory

† When working with Bill Arkwright, I came into contact with a Celtic witch from Ireland, who used a curse to kill a County landowner. We called her a banshee witch because she behaved like that elemental, the difference being that she brought about the death rather than just foretelling it. In addition to the curse—uttered in the Old Tongue—and the wailing cries, she used a ritual that involved washing and twisting a burial shroud. This caused the heart of the victim to rupture. —Tom Ward

The accurate use of words is vital, and sometimes the curse is actually written down and sent to the intended victim. In rare cases it is written on skin rather than parchment or paper.

A number of years ago, the three main Pendle clans, the Malkins, the Deanes, and the Mouldheels, came together and cursed me. The parchment they sent had spots of blood on it from victims who were probably murdered as part of the dark magical ritual. The leaders of the three covens also signed in blood. On the next page is that curse—which I must confess did cause me a few sleepless nights.

By screeching owl, by toad and bat,

By scuttling beetle, shiny black,

We curse thy soul! We'll take thy life!

By bloodred moon and starless sky,

By writhing bones and corpse's sigh,

We curse thy soul! We'll take thy life!

By slithering snake and long-tailed rat,

By mandrake root and familiar cat,

We curse thy soul! We'll take thy life!

These words have been written in the blood of innocents.

Thus cursed you are by covens three:

You will die in a dark place, far underground,

    with no friend at your side!

Darcie Malkin,

        Jessie Deane,

            & Claris Mouldheel

Many years have passed and the curse has still had no effect, but whenever my work calls me to venture underground, it always comes into my mind, and I am doubly on my guard.

Elemental Magic

At its most basic level, this form of magic is usually practiced by novice witches being trained within a clan, or unaware witches who frequent lonely places where they feel in tune with nature. The latter often sense a presence close by: unknown to them, this is an emerging elemental spirit, feeding and growing as a result of contact with a curious human mind. By focusing on the outcome she desires, the novice malevolent witch can use the power of the elemental to ill wish.

The elemental will do her bidding and exert its power against the chosen victim. Death rarely results from such a malignant partnership, but night terrors, ill health, and infestations of lice are common.

Used by skilled and experienced practitioners, elemental magic is very powerful. Fully developed elementals such as barghests and moroi are used both as guardians and killers. The latter in particular are a deadly threat in Romania, where, under the control of demons, they possess bears and attack their designated victims with terrible fury.

Familiar Magic

This is the most powerful of the three categories of magic used by the Pendle witches, although such practitioners may also use blood and bone magic from time to time. Magic of this type has tremendous and terrible potential.

The witch binds a creature to her will, at first feeding her own blood to her chosen familiar. Once it is bound to her, the blood of victims may be substituted. The creature effectively becomes an extension of the witch's own body. It is as if she can detach her hand and have it operate at a distance. It becomes her eyes and ears. The possibilities afforded by this dreadful magic are numerous and varied, depending on what type of creature a witch chooses as her familiar. Often witches have more than one, each suited to a different purpose. A cat can be used to spy on an enemy witch or scratch out her eyes, or even kill her

* The water witch
Morwena had
a corpse fowl as
her familiar.
She used it to
hunt for me on
Monastery Marsh.
It was slayed by
Grimalkin, the
witch assassin. —
Tom Ward

baby by sitting on its face and smothering it while it sleeps.

Bats and birds have the advantage of flight and can enable a witch to search for both enemies and victims. She usually chooses birds of the night, such as owls and corpse fowls.*

Cats, especially black ones, are probably the most popular familiars, and many witches choose them because of their own feline nature. Cats are quick and subtle, but also cruel: They play with their prey before devouring it.

Snakes are almost as common, not least because of their ability to kill. County snakes are not usually dangerous, but association with a witch increases the power of their jaws and endows them with a lethal venom they would not normally possess.

Toads are the least powerful of familiars, and are usually employed by very old, isolated witches (whose powers are waning and who merely want the latest gossip) and by those whose grasp of dark magic is extremely limited. However, they are the favorite familiars of water witches, well suited to the boggy terrain they inhabit, and their skin oozes a particularly virulent poison: The merest contact with it results in death.

Finally there are what we term higher-order familiars. These are entities such as demons that would normally be considered too dangerous and power-ful to be employed as familiars. Only the very strongest witches dare to attempt this, and few can carry it off. Almost inevitably there is a power struggle, and the witch may become subservient to that which she sought to control.*

* Alice Deane made a pact with the Bane, a very powerful spirit that had formerly been one of the Old Gods. In giving it her blood and attempting to bind it to her will, she was in effect making it her familiar. She was in great danger, but the fact that she was able to deal with it in such a way is a testimony to her power. Alice Deane must never be allowed to turn to the dark. — John Gregory

Mirrors and Scrying

There are three ways in which the Pendle witches combine dark magic with the use of mirrors.

1. To communicate over a distance, either by lip reading from one another's reflected images or by writing. Most witches are skilled at lip reading, but sometimes they write on the mirror when communicating with others unused to the practice. Using dark magic, they can locate another mirror and their message appears there. A very skillful witch can even use a puddle or any surface of calm water.

2. They use mirrors to spy on their enemies or victims. As a defense against that magical art, many inhabitants of the Pendle district turn their mirrors to the wall after dark.

3. Some witches believe that they have the ability to use mirrors to prophesy. Using the blood of a victim as ink, they draw magical symbols along the edges of a mirror. Afterward, spells are chanted, and they supposedly see visions of the future in the glass. Such so-called scryers are almost certainly deluded. I refuse to believe that

the future is fixed. Free will and choice shape what happens.*

Moon Magic

This type of magic is mostly practiced by benign witches. Practitioners sometimes dance naked at the time of the full moon to strengthen the power of the herbs they gather for healing.

The moon is said to show the truth of things, and can sometimes counter spells of false appearance.

Sniffing

Long sniffing is used by a witch to sniff out approaching danger.† Seventh sons of seventh sons are immune to that power, but we must still beware of short sniffing; up close, a witch can use it to find out our strengths and weaknesses. The nearer she approaches, the worse it gets. Always keep a witch at bay with a rowan staff, and above all, never let her breathe into your face!

† Bony Lizzie used long sniffing to foresee the danger from the Chipenden mob that eventually burned down her house. —Tom Ward

* Mab Mouldheel used mirrors twice, to my knowledge, to predict the future. In the first instance, she foretold the breaching of Malkin Tower and the threat to our lives by retreating witches. In the second, she foretold the near death of Alice Deane in Greece at the hands of a feral lamia. —Tom Ward

Spells of False Appearance

Otherwise known as dread, glamour, and fascination, these spells allow a malevolent witch to hide what she really is.

Dread is used to change her appearance in order to terrify her enemies. Instead of hair, a nest of black snakes may adorn her head and her eyes may glow red like fiery coals. Additionally, her face deforms and becomes monstrous.

Glamour and fascination work together. The former makes a witch seem younger and more beautiful than she really is; fascination then forces a man to

believe anything she tells him. He becomes like a rabbit in thrall to a stoat. But only the very strongest of witches can maintain such illusions in moonlight.

Sympathetic Magic

This type of magic is usually used to kill, cripple, or seriously hurt the enemy of a witch. A clay or wax figure is modeled in the shape of the intended victim. Into it are mixed ingredients that make it more potent, such as the victim's blood or urine. If these cannot be obtained, a strand of hair or a small piece of material from the victim's clothing will usually suffice.

What happens next is bounded only by the imagination and vindictiveness of the witch. Any injury inflicted on the figure will result in the victim feeling that pain. The witch has created sympathy between the figure and the living person. So a nail driven into any part of the model's anatomy will be felt in the same place on the living being. If the head and heart are targeted, then death will come swiftly. Alternatively, the victim may be crippled. Melting part of the model might result in a wasting disease.

A witch bottle is often used as a defense against an enemy witch who is already using dark magic. Some of her urine is placed in the bottle, along with sharp stones, pins, and iron nails. Once corked, the bottle is given a good shake, then left in the sun for three days. On the night of the next full moon it's buried under a dung heap. The next time the witch tries to urinate, she finds herself in agony. Thereupon the witch is informed of what has been done, and in return for halting her own magical attack, the witch bottle is destroyed.

DEALING WITH WITCHES

Unlike boggarts, witches cannot be confined using the power of salt and iron alone. But several techniques can be used to bind them successfully.

Symbols such as those sketched on the facing page are used to mark the pit of a bound witch. A Greek letter sigma is used to denote a sorceress, and a diagonal line sloping from right to left indicates a successful binding. Additionally, the type of witch (here the Greek letter lambda for lamia) and the ranking (1 being the most powerful) may be marked on the stone. It is vital to write the witch's full name below the symbols to identify her. Being women, they are subtle and may change over time. Each history must be consulted in my Chipenden library.

Finally, as with boggarts, the name of the spook who carried out the binding should be written directly under the witch's name.

Marcia Skelton
Gregory

Dealing with Dead Witches

Witches are sometimes hanged, then given to their families for burial, but this achieves little.

One problem when dealing with witches is that for most, death isn't the end of them. They are bone bound, their spirits trapped in their corpses, so if a witch is simply buried, one night she'll scratch her way to the surface and go hunting for victims and suck their blood to renew her strength.

Witches vary in power. A really strong witch might roam for miles in a single night; others can only drag themselves a few paces and often hide under moldering leaves, waiting for someone to pass close to their lair.*

* *Some witches are so strong that they can break free and be born into the world again. My master calls this reincarnation.—apprentice Bob Crosby*

Below are the important stages in the process of binding a dead witch.

1. Hire a master mason and a blacksmith. Both tradesmen should have previous experience of the task at hand. Set them to work constructing a stone-and-iron cover for the pit.

2. Dig a pit to contain the body of the witch. This should be a shaft nine feet deep and six feet long by three feet wide.

3. Next, ease the body into the pit headfirst. When night falls, unaware of her orientation, the dead witch will mistakenly dig herself deeper into the ground.

4. Next the mason and blacksmith must work together to construct the thirteen bars that will cover the pit, each bolted to a rim of stones.*

* In order to save money, some spooks place a large boulder over the witch's grave instead of iron bars. I would only use that as a temporary measure when dealing with a relatively weak witch. It's better to be safe than sorry. — John Gregory

Dealing with Live Witches

First, a malevolent witch must be captured;
This is best accomplished by use
of a silver chain. The technique
for casting the chain can only
be acquired by hours of
practice against targets:
My apprentice must test
his skills first against the
post in my garden, then
against moving targets. I also
practice regularly, as it wouldn't do
to let these skills get rusty. Below are
the general principles involved.

1. The silver chain should be coiled about
   the left wrist.

2. It should be cast with a twisting
   upward motion of the hand so that it
   spins widdershins, against the clock.

3. Enough elevation should be gained
   so that it drops over the witch,
   tightening as it falls, but not enough
   that she has time to evade it.

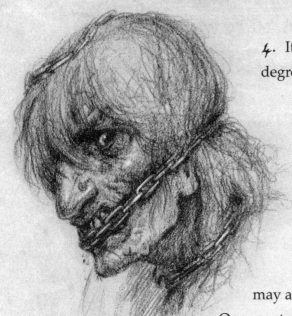

4. It is important to achieve a degree of what we call spread. This means that the chain should bind the witch from head to knee. With sufficient practice, it is possible to ensure that the chain tightens against her teeth. Her silence is desirable. She may attempt to use dark magic. Once captured, the witch must be dealt with. Burning, cruel though it is, destroys the witch for all time. Another good method is to eat the heart of the witch. This barbarous but reliable method is not usually practiced in the County, but some spooks kill a witch, then feed her heart to their dogs.* One other reliable method of dealing with a witch—the one I use—is to keep her in a pit reinforced with iron bars.

* I was sent to work with Bill Arkwright for six months. He was a hard man who beat me badly on two occasions. One of the worst things I ever witnessed was the killing of a water witch that he'd had imprisoned in a pit for two years. She was still screaming when he threw her heart to his dogs.—apprentice Jack Farington

Mother Malkin, one of the strongest witches the County has ever seen, possessed the body of a pig butcher. After she was driven out by salt and iron, her heart was devoured by pigs. —Tom Ward

When the witch Wurmalde died, dropped by a vaengir lamia from a great height onto Gore Rock in Pendle, the Spook told me that her slayer had already ripped out her heart and devoured it. —Tom Ward

Below are the important stages of the process of binding a live witch in a pit.

1. Hire a master mason and a blacksmith. Both tradesmen should be reliable and experienced. They should also have strong nerves because dealing with a live witch can be *very* dangerous.

2. Dig the pit. This should be nine feet deep, six feet wide, and six feet long.

3. With a strong witch, line the walls with a mixture of salt and iron. Leave the floor of the pit clear so that she can survive on a diet of slugs and insects. When dealing with feral lamias or water witches, a cage of iron bars needs to be constructed and buried in the ground (both types of witch can burrow).

4. The critical point is getting the witch into the pit. The silver chain should bind her until the very last moment. The skill lies in rolling the witch into the pit, simultaneously uncoiling the chain. This can only be learned by practice.

5. Finally, stay in attendance until the mason and smith have sealed the pit.

This technique has one serious but fortunately rare drawback. After being kept in a pit for many years, eating slugs and worms, the water seeping into her flesh and bones, an extremely strong witch starts to change. If she is then killed, she will become wick–not only able to move her body great distances, but soft and pliable, with the ability to squeeze into a tiny space. Entering a human body through the nose or ears, the witch can possess it and use it for her own purposes.

The difficulty then is to identify the witch, but there are two ways: A body that is newly possessed has poor balance and may stagger as if dizzy or even completely lose its balance and fall over. There are often personality changes, too. Someone who was formerly kind, calm, and happy may suddenly become excitable and bad tempered.*

* As a young man, I wrote the definitive guide to possession. It is to be found in my Chipenden library and is titled The Damned, the Dizzy, and the Desperate. — John Gregory

A Kehalos

MAGES

Human mages are the male counterparts of witches and may also be placed in the same categories—the benign, the falsely accused, the malevolent, and the unaware—but they are relatively few in number, the use of dark magic coming more naturally to the female. With the exception of goat mages (see page 148) they work alone.

The only nonhuman mages that have come to my attention are the Kobalos, and there is some doubt about their actual existence (see page 150). But if the report I've heard proves to be true, one day they may pose a dangerous threat to the County as they wander farther south toward our shores.

Like witches, whatever the type of magecraft they practice, each mage varies in ability. The weakest may be no more than fairground conjurors faking most of their tricks to take coins from gullible audiences; the strongest may rule a kingdom, although often they are the hidden power behind a throne.

Mages tend to use longer and more complicated spells than witches, reading them aloud from a grimoire. They also use a pentacle, a circle encompassing a five-pointed star, at each point of which is placed a black wax candle. Such pentacles must be drawn very precisely, and the magical symbols within must also be accurate; the survival of the mage depends upon it.

He may stand at its center, safe from the demon, or Old God, that materializes beyond its protecting boundary. The danger here is that the conjured entity —brought from the dark against its will—may take revenge on innocent people nearby. Sometimes this is deliberate, the conjuring a premeditated act of violence against the mage's enemies.

The safer alternative is when the mage stands outside the pentacle and conjures the entity to appear within it, where it is bound until dismissed.

DEALING WITH MAGES

When dealing with live mages, the techniques used to slay or confine witches usually prove successful— except for salt and iron, which have no effect at all.

A malevolent mage is a servant of the dark and may be bound with a silver chain or slain with a silver-alloy blade. Rowan wood can also cause some mages severe pain, while others have a tolerance for it. A spook has some degree of immunity against magecraft, but the struggle can become physical: When threatened, most mages quickly resort to extreme violence.

Unlike witches, dead malevolent mages are not bone bound and cannot leave their graves. Their spirits pass through limbo to their natural home in the dark. Some mages do live extraordinarily long lives, and indeed much of their magic is designed to achieve that end; while malevolent witches accept death through natural old age, knowing they have a physical existence beyond the grave where they will still be able to satisfy their blood lust.

MERLIN

Merlin is perhaps the most famous mage of all, the power behind the throne of Arthur, a warlike Celtic king. Merlin had a human mother, but his father was reportedly a demon, and from him he inherited magical powers, including the ability to shift his shape into different people or even animals.

In later life he increased his existing power by learning to use the energy of a dragon, which is a very dangerous thing to do. He then fell in love with the witch Nimueh, who pried out his magical secrets, drained him of power, and used it against him. She trapped Merlin within the aura of a powerful

Merlin

dragon. He still sleeps and will remain there until the
end of the world.

*Once again it must be stressed that it is very dangerous to trust a woman—especially a witch. There are
many good women in the world, but even when dealing with a benign witch, never tell her everything: always
hold something in reserve.* — *John Gregory*

TYPES OF MAGES

Goat Mages

Goat mages dwell in Ireland and derive their power
through Pan magic, routinely sacrificing goats to that

Old God.* The idea is that, through worship and blood letting, Pan will grant them power. Fortunately, Pan is unreliable, and the mage is more likely to be driven insane. When, on occasion, Pan does reward the mage, the power received is used with unpredictable and devastating effects. (Pan magic is akin to madness.)

Goat mages have a major annual event, which is very sinister and dangerous. A goat is tethered to a high platform and worshipped for a week and a day. Human beings are sacrificed to the cloven-hoofed creature, which is gradually possessed by Pan, the horned god. Soon the goat acquires the power of speech, stands upon its hind legs, and grows larger, dominating the proceedings and demanding more and more sacrifices.

* This type of magic is rarely practiced by witches.
— John Gregory

A Goat Mage

The power derived from those eight days of bloodshed lasts the mages for almost a year. Some years Pan is not contacted and the mages must flee, scattering themselves to the winds. They are then totally vulnerable, and their enemies, a federation of landowners to the southwest of that land, hunt them down. But in a good year, when their power is in the ascendancy, they are greatly feared. Then they travel unchecked, seek out their enemies, and put them to death, stealing their land and wealth. The goat mages and the federation are in a perpetual state of war.

Kobalos Mages

The Kobalos are not human. They walk upright but have the appearance of a fox or a wolf. The body is covered with dark hair; the face and hands are shaved according to custom; and the mage wears a long black coat with a slit in the back to accommodate his tail, which can function as an extra limb.

These mages are solitary creatures who shun their fellow citizens and usually dwell beyond the fringes of the frozen Kobalos domain, which is far to the north of the continent known as Europa. Each one "farms" a haizda, a territory that he has marked out as his own. Within it there are several hundred humans, living in hamlets, villages, and farms. He rules by fear and magecraft, harvesting souls and accumulating power. He usually lives in an old, gnarled ghanbala tree, sleeping by day but traveling the boundaries of his haizda by night, taking the blood of humans and animals for sustenance. He can shift his shape, taking on the appearance of animals, and can also vary his size. This type of mage is also a formidable warrior whose favorite weapon is a sabre.

The Kobalos are a fierce, warlike race who, with the exception of their mages, inhabit Valkarky, a city deep within the arctic circle.

The name Valkarky means the City of the Petrified Tree; it is filled with all types of abominations that have been created by dark magic. Its walls are constructed

The Kobalos

and renewed by creatures that never sleep; creatures that spit soft stone from their mouths. The Kobalos believe that their city will not stop growing until it covers the entire world.*

Necromancers

While a spook deals with the unquiet dead as a routine part of his job, talking to them and sending them on their way to the light, a necromancer does the opposite.[†] He often uses a grimoire, a book of spells and rituals, and binds the dead so that they serve his purposes and help him to line his pockets with silver. The bereaved will pay hard-earned money for a brief conversation—or even a glimpse of their loved ones.

He also uses the dead as spies and to terrorize his enemies. Most often it is just a case of trapping graveside lingerers, or those bound to their bones, because they've committed some terrible crime.

---

* The above is based upon the writings of a very early spook called Nicholas Browne, who traveled far beyond the borders of the County. Apart from his notebooks, there is no evidence that any of his assertions are true, but we must keep an open mind. The world is a big place and much remains to be explored. — John Gregory

[†] The word necromancer comes from the Greek nekros, which means corpse. —apprentice Mark Caster

152

Rarely, some very powerful necromancers can trap the dead in limbo and stop them from reaching the light; they can then summon them at will into the presence of the living. Initially this is done by means of a pentacle, which is chalked on the floor, making sure that all five points of the star are of equal length and that a black candle* is positioned upon each one. After the correct spell has been cast, reading accurately from the grimoire, the lost soul appears in the pentacle and is trapped there until the necromancer has completed further spells of binding.† The soul is then dismissed and goes back into limbo, with no chance of finding its way to the light. After this, the pentacle is no longer required and the necromancer can summon the ghost to his side with a simple command.

* The black candles are identical to those used by malevolent witches in their rituals. Bony Lizzie had them in her house when I rescued the child called Tommy. I've seen them many times since, and their presence is always a bad sign. Their dark color is achieved by mixing human blood into the wax. —Tom Ward

† My master's ex-apprentice, Morgan, turned from the light and practiced necromancy. In return for money, he summoned the dead from limbo for grieving families. Even worse, he trapped the spirit of my own father and made him believe that he was burning in Hell. —Tom Ward

MORGAN'S FIRST ATTEMPT TO RAISE GOLGOTH

My apprentice Morgan had many faults, but the two worst were
laziness and an extreme lust for power. He was approaching the
end of the third year of his apprenticeship when he attempted
something that could have had terrible consequences for the
inhabitants of the County and beyond.

At the time he was tall and strong for his sixteen years, and
already giving me much cause for concern. As well as the two
serious faults listed above, he was rebellious and imperious,
always believing that he was right. It all came to a head when we
were staying at my winter house in Anglezarke.

The Hursts, a family who had fostered Morgan until he was almost thirteen, also lived nearby, and theirs was a tragic tale. Within a year of his return, he and their daughter Eveline had fallen in love. Although they weren't blood relatives, the parents considered them to be brother and sister and reacted violently, beating both children and making their lives unbearable. As a result, the distraught Eveline drowned herself in the miserable stretch of gray water that borders their farm.

Morgan was the seventh son of a seventh son and the daughter of a woman called Emily Burns, whom I'd once been very close to. So as a favor to her, and to help Morgan and get him away from that dreadful situation, where his adoptive parents held

him responsible for their daughter's death, I took him on as my apprentice. It proved to be one of the biggest mistakes of my long life.

During our winter visits to Anglezarke, unlikely though it might seem, Morgan seemed to grow closer to the Hursts. He took to visiting them at Moor View Farm and even spent the occasional night there. I didn't object, thinking that his presence might afford them some consolation. Perhaps they'd realized that they had played a part in causing Eveline to take her own life and were trying to make amends in some way.

I was careless—I realize that now. The boy often wandered onto the bleak moor and was obsessed by an ancient burial mound called the Round Loaf. Beneath it, supposedly, was a secret chamber where the ancients once worshipped one of the Old Gods. This deity was Golgoth, the Lord of Winter, and it was believed that the meddling of those ancient priests as they tried to raise their god brought about the last Ice Age, when Golgoth had stayed in our world, freezing it in the grip of an extended winter that had resulted in thousands of deaths.

I'd caught Morgan digging into the mound more than once. He didn't find the secret chamber then but discovered something else that I hadn't even suspected was there. Morgan had been preparing for months to attempt a terrible summoning; as his master, I failed to guess the danger. As a spook, I must confess that I failed the County.

*

Late one winter's night there was a loud rapping on the back door of my winter house; on the doorstep was Mr. Hurst, wrapped up well against the snow that was beginning to whirl down out of the dark clouds above.

"Come inside, man, before you freeze to death!" I cried, welcoming him into the kitchen. "What brings you out on such a night?"

The walk up from the farm was difficult in winter, but when a blizzard threatened, it was dangerous to life. Even someone with a lifetime of local knowledge might get lost in the snow, which would mean certain death before morning.

"We need you back at the farm quickly!" Mr Hurst told me. "Something terrible's happening. . . ." At that, his jaw clamped shut and his whole body began to tremble.

"Take your time," I said, sitting him down on a stool close to the fire and handing him the cup of the hot broth I'd prepared for my supper. "Your need may be urgent, but I must know exactly what I'm dealing with."

So, as the old farmer sipped his broth and got some warmth back into his bones, he began to tell his tale.

"It's that daft lad Morgan," he said. "He's locked himself in his room and is up to no good. He's using dark magic, I'm sure of it!"

"His bedroom?" I asked.

"Nay, the front room, where he writes things in his notebook and does his reading."

"'Reading? What reading?" I asked. Writing up what he'd

learned in his notebook was only to be expected, but I brought
few books with me from Chipenden to my cold, damp house on
Anglezarke Moor; those I did were kept in the warmest room
and rarely allowed out of my sight. My books are precious to
me, a store of knowledge that I fear to lose.

"He came home with a big leather book a few weeks ago, and
he's hardly had his nose out of it since. But tonight he locked
himself in the room. First he carried a sack in there; then he
dragged the farm dog in. Now he won't answer the door, and the
poor animal keeps whining. It sounds terrified out of its skin.
There are other sounds, too. And the whole house seems to be
getting really cold despite all the logs we heap on the fire. Our
breath is steaming and ice is forming on the outside of the door
of Morgan's room."

"What other sounds are there?" I cried, jumping to my feet.
Suddenly I'd glimpsed how great the danger might be.

"Bells keep ringing. Not small bells. One sounds like a big
church bell, so loud that the wooden floors vibrate with each
peal. And from time to time there's a deep grinding sound that
seems to come from right under the house."

At last, convinced of the need for urgency, I wasted no
further time in leading Mr. Hurst out into the night. We headed
down the steep clough and onto the slope that led off the snow-
clad moor. White flakes were dancing into our faces, and it was
bitterly cold. It was a good hour before we had finally trudged
across to Moor View Farm. No sooner had we crossed the

threshold than I realized that the old farmer had not exaggerated.
The farmhouse was unnaturally cold, that strange chill that warns
us spooks that something from the dark is close at hand.

As we approached the locked room, I heard an unnerving
sound from deep beneath the house: a grinding, crunching,
grating roar, as if some huge beast were munching on rock.
We both became still, feeling the boards move beneath our feet.
When the noise subsided, I rapped hard on the door and called
out Morgan's name loudly.

There was no reply. On the outside of the wooden door,
rivulets of ice had formed. Suddenly the noise began again,
as if some monster were rising up from the depths beneath,
clawing aside rocks and earth in its eagerness to be free of its
subterranean prison.

I threw my shoulder against the door again and again,
desperation lending me strength. At last the hinges sheered away
from the wood and the door burst open. I stepped into a cold
more severe than that on the bleak moor from which we'd just
descended.

I'd been in that room before and knew its layout. Longer
than it was wide, it had one window on the far wall, shrouded
with heavy black curtains. There was a big table with two chairs;
these usually occupied the center of the room, but now they'd
been pushed right back against the wall. Morgan was sitting
inside a huge pentacle that he had chalked on the floor. At each
of its five outer points was a black candle. Their yellow

flickering light filled the room and showed me exactly what
I was dealing with.

In his left hand Morgan held a grimoire, a book of dark
magic incantations. It was bound in green leather, and there was
a silver pentacle embossed on its cover. Where he had gotten it
from I didn't know, but he was chanting from it, reading words
in the Old Tongue—the language of the ancients who first
made their home in the County. His accent was far from perfect,
but close enough to make the incantation potent, and although
it was invisible, I sensed that something was taking shape just
beyond the pentacle, between Morgan and the dark curtains
at the window.

Behind me, in the open doorway, I heard Mrs. Hurst scream
with fright, and her husband give a deep groan of pure terror. I
too was very afraid, but something greater than fear for my own
safety urged me forward and gave me the courage I needed. It was
a realization of what threatened; the knowledge that the whole

County was just a few seconds away from a disaster of almost unimaginable proportions.

There was one other creature in the room: the farm dog. It was chained to a hook in the wall just by the curtains. Flat on its belly, its ears back against its skull, the poor animal was whining softly and trembling all over. The dog was the blood sacrifice that Morgan was offering in order to bring Golgoth into our world. He was trying to raise the Lord of Winter and had almost succeeded.

The cold intensified, blasting toward me; it felt as if sharp knives were cutting into my face. But although my foolish apprentice was far closer to the emerging Old God, he was protected by the pentacle.

I ran forward and kicked over one of the candles, thus destroying its protective power. Immediately Morgan's eyes widened as he felt the first icy fingers of cold reach toward him. But lust for power had filled him with madness, and although he rose to his feet, he continued to chant from the grimoire.

I stepped inside the pentacle and struck his wrists hard with my staff. The book flew from his hands. He stared at me, his expression a mixture of anger, bewilderment, and fear. For a moment he seemed in a trance, unaware of who he was or what he was trying to do. But then his eyes widened in alarm and he looked across to where Golgoth had begun to materialize.

Again that roaring filled the house, the bare stone flags beneath our feet beginning to move. As the noise reached its climax, the dog gave a shrill cry, shuddered, and lay still. It was dead—not because Golgoth had touched it with his cold deadly fingers. It had died of fright.

Gradually the noises subsided, the cold began to lessen, and the fear that had been squeezing my heart slowly released its grip. I had knocked the grimoire from Morgan's hand before he could complete the ritual. Golgoth had been forced to return to the dark. For now, the County was safe.

It was the end of Morgan's apprenticeship to me. I couldn't keep him on after he'd done that. I should really have bound him in a pit. After all, I do that to witches. But his mother begged me not to, and I relented. He turned fully to the dark after that.*

* Morgan tried to raise Golgoth a second time and succeeded. However, it cost him his life. It was a horrific death that I will never forget. —Tom Ward

Shamans

A shaman uses animism magic and employs the spirit of an animal as his familiar. He feeds it some of his life essence in return for its guidance and protection. Using this, a shaman projects his soul from his body and can venture far in the twinkling of an eye; in addition to his journeys to earthly locations, he routinely ventures into limbo. One famous shaman called Lucius Grim crossed over to the domain of the dark several times, until his soul was finally devoured by a demon. His body continued to breathe for many years afterward, but it was just an empty vessel.

Not all shamans are malevolent. Using their animal spirit, some practice healing; others attempt to control the weather, bringing rainfall to alleviate droughts.

Grimoires

These are ancient books, full of spells and rituals, used to invoke the dark. Sometimes they are employed by witches, but they are mainly used by mages, and their spells have to be followed to the letter, or death can result.*

* Mr. Gregory keeps a grimoire in the locked writing desk of his Anglezarke house. I once saw him reading it and asked him why it was there. He told me to mind my own business.—apprentice Andy Cuerden

Many of these famous texts have been lost (the *Patrixa* and the *Key of Solomon*). The most dangerous and powerful grimoires, however, were written in the Old Tongue by the first men of the County. Primarily used to summon demons, these books contain terrible dark magic. Most have been deliberately destroyed or hidden far from human sight.

The most mysterious, and reputedly most deadly, of these is the *Doomdryte*. Some believe that this book was dictated word for word by the Fiend to a mage called Lukrasta. That grimoire contains just one long dark magic incantation. If successfully completed (in conjunction with certain rituals), it would allow a mage to achieve immortality, invulnerability, and godlike powers.

Fortunately no one has ever succeeded, as it requires intense concentration and great endurance: The book takes thirteen hours to read aloud, and you cannot pause for rest.

One word mispronounced brings about the immediate death of the mage. Lukrasta was the first to attempt the ritual, and the first to die. Others followed in his foolish footsteps.

We must hope that the *Doomdryte* remains lost forever.

The Pendle witches have their own grimoires,

but they never contain the ritual for summoning the Fiend. They consider this too dangerous to be written down: it is learned by heart and passed down through the clans from mother to daughter.*

*Alice told me that Bony Lizzie owned three grimoires, but they were destroyed by fire when a mob attacked their dwelling near Chipenden.
—Tom Ward

The Ghasts on Hangman's Hill

THE UNQUIET DEAD

The unquiet dead form a large part of the work carried out by spooks. Being seventh sons of seventh sons, we can see and hear the dead and have conversations with their spirits. Ghasts we can do nothing about (see page 171), but with ghosts our rate of success is high.

Unlike priests, who try to exorcise ghosts using the ritual of bell, book, and candle, we talk directly to them, as you would to a living person. Our first priority is to find out why they have become trapped on earth. This is usually a consequence of some crime they have committed or their own sudden violent death. Many do not even realize they are dead. After convincing them that this is so, the next step is to persuade them to think of a happy memory from their former life. Concentration upon that usually solves the problem and gives them sufficient peace of mind to be able to find their way through the mists of limbo to the light.

The art of speaking to the dead must be practiced and the necessary skills developed. Some spooks are better at this than others. To be effective in this regard, we must empathize with ghosts and understand their pain and disorientation.*

SYMBOLS USED FOR THE UNQUIET DEAD

These are usually marked close to where the spirit lurks, perhaps carved into a tree or door. A Greek letter gamma (see opposite) is used for both ghosts and ghasts. The type of spirit is indicated at the top right. In this case, the letter sigma labels it as a strangler ghost.

Note the ranking system used: to the bottom right of the main symbol is a number; ranks 1 to 5 are ghosts; 6 to 10 are ghasts. In the example here, the strangler is a rank 3.

* Having completed my training as a spook, I was very disappointed to be unable to send the ghosts of my mam and dad to the light. Abe died in an accident; Amelia killed herself because she could not bear to live on alone. Still they haunt the mill. I have returned to Chipenden to ask my former master, John Gregory, to see if he can do anything for them. — Bill Arkwright

I tried my best but could not send them to the light. The dead husband could leave but refuses to do so without his wife. For some reason all my skill and experience in dealing with such matters proved useless. — John Gregory

The water witch Morwena revealed that the Fiend had prevented Arkwright's mam, Amelia, from going to the light. That explains why all the efforts to free her came to nothing. Then I bargained with the Fiend, agreeing to go out onto the marsh and face Morwena if, in exchange, he would release Amelia's soul. Now at last she and her husband, Abe, are at peace. —Tom Ward

Abhuman spirits are indicated by the Greek letter alpha. They are not classified into types, but a ranking is given from 1 to 10.

Abhuman Spirits

Abhuman spirits are human souls that have degenerated and fallen so far from their former condition that they are more akin to beasts, sometimes taking the form of hybrids, half human, half animal. This is often a result of spending a long time trapped in limbo or having committed some terrible crime on earth.

An Abhuman

A Group of Abhumans

Although a spirit can usually be persuaded to go to the light by focusing upon a happy memory of its former life, this always proves far more difficult when dealing with abhuman spirits. Often they cannot remember much of their existence on earth, much less any brief periods of happiness.

Most of these poor unfortunates cannot be helped by a spook and are doomed to exist in that tormented condition until the end of time itself. Nevertheless, if the opportunity presents itself, it is still worth making the effort to free them from that miserable existence.*

Ghasts

Ghasts are fragments of spirits that have been able to move on to the light only by leaving the evil part of themselves behind. Their behavior is repetitive and compulsive: Over and over again they repeat some act that they once performed when they were alive. Often it is a crime such as murder, but occasionally they are the victims.

* *Within the Ord, the citadel of the Ordeen, I saw a large number of abhuman spirits. They had degenerated as a result of passing back and forth between this world and the realm of the dark. It would have been impossible to free them by the usual means of talking them through to the light. — John Gregory*

The largest ghast visitation in the County takes place on Hangman's Hill, where, after a savage battle during their civil war, a large number of soldiers were executed. They can sometimes be seen there, hanging from the trees as they slowly choke to death.*

Ghasts feed upon terror. It makes them stronger. They are ranked from 6 to 10. Most people would be hardly aware of a 10, but those of the highest rank sometimes drive people insane from pure fear. Sometimes they try to touch the living with their cold fingers or even squeeze the throat or press on the chest to make breathing difficult.

The house in Horshaw, where I was born, harbors the ghast of a miner in the cellar. As soon as their training commences, I take all my apprentices there to see if they have sufficient courage to face the dark. I also attempt from time to time to deal with ghasts myself, but so far without success. As yet a spook can do nothing about such entities, and we must continue

---

* As a child, I was terrified by the ghasts on that hill. I could hear them swinging on the branches and choking as they hanged. When it got really bad and I couldn't sleep, my mam went alone up the hill and made them quiet for more than a month, something that not even a spook can do. —Tom Ward

to search for a way to get rid of them. It is fortunate that they fade slowly over time, eventually disappearing altogether.

Ghosts

Ghosts are full spirits still trapped on earth and unable to pass on, either because they are victims or have committed some heinous crime. Some may be bound to the scene of their crime; some to their own grave. Occasionally they have a message for those still alive and may linger for years, waiting for the opportunity to pass this on.

Ghosts are ranked from 1 to 5; strangler ghosts are always ranked from 1 to 3. A rank 1 strangler, although rare, is extremely dangerous and can asphyxiate its victims. Ghosts can choose whether or not to make themselves visible.

There are, very rarely, other visitations from beyond the grave. These never make themselves directly visible but sometimes cast a shadow. More usually there is a noise in the air—a cracking or tearing sound, as if the very fabric of our world is being ripped asunder and an entrance created. Very occasionally there is a physical sensation of warmth that announces the presence. I have never experienced such a phenomenon myself but have spoken to other spooks who have, and I'm convinced of the truth of such encounters. I suspect that such visitations come directly from the light and are both powerful and benign.*

* On the way back from Greece on board the Celeste, I had such an experience. I believe it was Mam returning briefly to say good-bye and let me know that she was all right. —Tom Ward

A CONVERSATION WITH A STRANGLER GHOST

In the third year after the death of my master, Henry Horrocks, I was summoned to Balderstone to deal with a suspected strangler ghost. Three deaths had occurred in less than a year, in a hamlet that had only forty remaining inhabitants. I was able to view the most recent corpse but was unable to interrogate its spirit, which had already moved on to the light.

Only rarely can strangler ghosts kill people; I knew that if this was what I was dealing with, then it must be exceptionally powerful, because it had exerted enough pressure to actually leave finger marks on the victim's throat. And there was a chance that the murderer was human. There are many examples in the County records of killers who have attempted to blame supernatural agencies for the deaths they have been charged with. But in this case all the victims had died on the western edge of the hamlet, close to a small dell, and that's where I eventually found the strangler.

There was no moon and the night was dark, with heavy cloud cover and hardly a breath of wind. I saw the ghost as a faint column of light moving through the trees toward the village. The strangler was no doubt seeking out its next victim. When I called out to it, the column of light halted and then proceeded swiftly in my direction. No doubt it thought I'd be easy prey. Stranglers and other ghosts are deterred by groups of people and are always more likely to manifest themselves to lone humans.

When it was no more than a staff's length away, it halted for a moment, at which point it became aware that I was not the easy victim it had anticipated. Nonetheless it attacked me, and I felt it place its cold fingers around my throat. It tried to choke me, but a seventh son of a seventh son has a degree of immunity, and it lacked the strength to do me any serious harm. So I tried to talk to it.

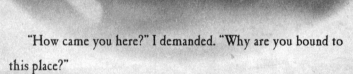

"How came you here?" I demanded. "Why are you bound to this place?"

"Love this dark dell," replied the strangler. "Killed many here before they caught me. Three women, a child, and an old man. Put my hands around their necks and squeezed until they struggled no more. But they caught me at last. . . ."

"Did you hang?"

"Nay. They kicked me with their heavy boots until all my bones were broken. Battered me until my spirit fled my body to escape the pain. Here I am now. Can't go too far from this place, but it's not so bad. Not so bad at all. Three I've taken in the last few months. So good, it is. So nice to put my cold fingers around warm plump necks!"

"You must leave here now," I warned him. "Each life you take only makes it harder for you. Go to the light. Go now while you still can!"

"What chance have I got of ever reaching the light?" the strangler asked in a melancholy voice.

"It's difficult, but it can be done," I explained. "Think of a happy memory. The moment on this earth when you were most happy!"

There was silence for over a minute; then at last the strangler spoke. "I remember one summer's morning when I was hardly higher than my mam's knee. She'd just given me a good slapping for doing something wrong—I can't remember what—when I saw a large butterfly hovering over a clump of long-stemmed dog daisies. It had red wings that shone in the sunlight, and I remember feeling so jealous that it should look that way when I was ugly and misshapen myself—my mam always said I should never have been born. It just didn't seem fair that it should be able to fly as well, when all I could do was hobble about.

"So when it settled on a flower head, I seized it quickly and pulled off both its wings. That showed it! Now it was just an ugly little insect and couldn't fly. I felt happier and better than I had in a long time. Aye, I remember that morning well. It taught me how I could make myself feel better by hurting others."

At that, I knew that the strangler was beyond salvation. Part of me felt sorry for that poor twisted spirit. It sounded as if he had endured a difficult childhood. But others are afflicted by worse and yet still rise above their pain. My duty was clear.

"Look toward the light!" I cried. "You should be able to see it now . . ."

"I can't see the light. Just a gray swirling mist . . ."

"Enter the mist and you'll find it. The light is just beyond it. Do it now!"

Within moments the column of light faded. But I had tricked it. The ghost was too tainted by its evil ways to ever reach the light. I had sent it off into the gray mists of limbo. The light did indeed lie beyond that region—I hadn't lied about that. But the strangler ghost had no hope of reaching it and would wander in limbo, perhaps for all eternity. It was cruel, but it had to be done. My first duty is always to the County and its inhabitants. No more people would die in that dell at the hands of the strangler.

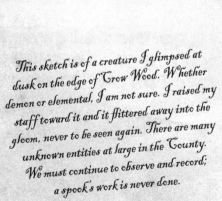

This sketch is of a creature I glimpsed at dusk on the edge of Crow Wood. Whether demon or elemental, I am not sure. I raised my staff toward it and it flittered away into the gloom, never to be seen again. There are many unknown entities at large in the County. We must continue to observe and record; a spook's work is never done.

— John Gregory

The Minotaur

DEMONS

Demons, like boggarts, are spirit entities, but they are much more powerful and intelligent. They have complete control of their shape and appearance, becoming visible or invisible at will. They also have highly developed language skills. Some of them aspire to be gods, like the Old Gods, and spend their time trying to augment their power at the expense of their human victims. The stronger ones want to be worshipped.

They do not dwell in the dark like the Old Gods, who pass into our world through portals. Demons are bound to this world, usually frequenting a particular location from which they cannot wander far.* Although they are less powerful than the Old Gods, they can be extremely dangerous.

* The main exception to this rule is the demons that pass to and fro from the dark to our world through the fiery portal used by the Ordeen. It is the power of that goddess that makes such a thing possible.
— John Gregory

Bugganes

The buggane is a category of demon that frequents ruins and usually materializes as a black bull or a hairy man, although other forms are chosen if they suit its purpose. In marshy ground, bugganes have been known to shape shift into wormes (see under Water Beasts, page 200).

The buggane makes two distinctive sounds—either bellowing like an enraged bull to warn off those who venture near its domain, or whispering to its victims in a sinister human voice. It tells the afflicted that it is sapping their life force, and their terror lends the demon even greater strength. Covering one's ears is

A Buggane

no protection—the voice of the buggane is heard right inside the head. Even the profoundly deaf have been known to fall victim to its insidious sound. Those who hear the whisper die within days unless they slay the buggane first. It stores the life force (see Animism Magic, page 120) of each person it slays in a labyrinth, which it constructs far underground.

Bugganes are immune to salt and iron, which makes them hard to kill and to confine. The only thing they are vulnerable to is a blade made from silver alloy, which must be driven into the heart of the buggane when it has fully materialized.

Another source of their strength is the alliance they sometimes make with witches or mages: In return for human sacrifices, they will destroy an enemy.

They are most common on the Isle of Mona, which lies to the northwest of the County coast, where a particularly dangerous one haunts a ruined chapel at the foot of Greeba Mountain. Bugganes, like some types of boggart, are occasionally open to persuasion or may be prepared to move location in exchange for something they badly want.

Harpies

These are said to be female; they are winged, and descend upon their prey faster than a stone falls

Harpies

through the air. The only warning that they are heading in your direction is a stench that is carried toward the victim no matter which way the wind is blowing. Sent out by Zeus, the former leader of the Old Gods, they hunt down those who have displeased him, to rend and tear them apart with their sharp claws. The bodies of the slain are contaminated by their visit, along with the surrounding land; plants and animals die, and nothing will grow in the soil there for many decades afterward.

These observations were recorded from the ancient writings of the Greek spooks, but it seems likely to me that harpies never existed. Sightings of flying lamias probably gave birth to this legend. Without evidence we must always be skeptical. Note also that Zeus is no longer the leader of the Old Gods and through lack of worship has declined in power.

Kelpies

The kelpie is a type of malevolent demon that lives in rivers and lakes and has a great hunger for human flesh. It's a shape shifter that usually takes the form of a black horse or pony. It allows a human to ride on

A Kelpie

its back before galloping into the water to drown him. If particularly hungry, it bites off the feet of its victim.

The kelpie loves extreme weather conditions and often manifests itself during thunderstorms, when it shape shifts into a very hairy man, leaps out of the water and crushes its victim to death, snapping every bone in the process. Whether in the form of a man or a horse, however, a kelpie's teeth are barbed and slope backward. Once it has bitten into flesh, it is almost impossible to pry its jaws open. A kelpie can be bound with a silver chain—though only with difficulty, because of its great agility. Like other demons, it is vulnerable to a silver blade.

Selkies

Selkies are water demons and usually live in the sea, appearing in the shape of a seal. But they can also take the form of a beautiful woman and live on land undetected. In this guise, selkies have been known to live with an unsuspecting man for years at a time. Selkies are benign creatures and like music, particularly sad songs. They are essentially lonely and thrive on human companionship. But they age very slowly indeed, and if one does choose to live with a man, her youth can attract the attention of neighbors, particularly jealous women. Although harmless in themselves, their presence makes people uneasy and nervous, given that they are a type of demon. Then a spook may be called in to help.

The best way to deal with a selkie is to hunt the creature, usually with dogs, which attempt to catch it and tear it to pieces. If the selkie escapes, she returns to the sea and again takes on the shape of a seal.*

Strigoi and Strigoica

Strigoi are masculine; strigoica are feminine. These vampiric (blood-drinking) demons live in Romania, mostly in the province of Transylvania. Often content to exist for years in spirit form, many eventually choose to possess the living; when their host dies, they move on to seize another body. Others prefer to animate the dead and choose a corpse soon after it has been buried.

* Seconded to Bill Arkwright, I helped hunt down a selkie far to the north of the County. Bill's poor dog followed it into the water and was seized and drowned. After killing the dog, the selkie escaped.—apprentice Graham Cain

Working with Bill Arkwright, I was also witness to the hunting of a selkie. The creature was living happily with a fisherman in the shape of a woman, and it seemed cruel and unjust that she should be driven into the sea, leaving him alone. The poor man was distraught. There are some jobs a spook shouldn't have to do. —Tom Ward

These demons enter a living host through a cut or wound. Romanians are so fearful of this that they will endure the pain of cauterization—the wound being burned with a hot poker to seal it against that threat. The dead have no defense, and strigoi and strigoica follow wormholes into a corpse.

Strigoi and strigoica demons often work in pairs. One animates a living host, guarding and protecting the other during daylight hours. Many live in grand, isolated dwellings and have accumulated wealth acquired from the living hosts they have possessed.

Once clothed in human form, living or dead, they exist on a diet of human blood, but sometimes eat raw flesh, hearts and livers being considered particular delicacies.

A Strigoi

It is the practice of Romanian spooks to dig up bodies one year after they have been interred. If decomposition is under way, the corpse is considered to be free of possession. However, if it has changed little— and especially if the face is pink or red and the lips swollen—it is deemed to be possessed by vampiric demons and the head is cut off and burned.

There are many ways to deal with strigoi and strigoica, both the living and the dead: They can be decapitated; a stake may be driven through the left eye; or they can be burned. They also can be kept at bay using garlic, roses, and the same method employed against water witches—a salt-filled water moat. Only a demon possessing a dead body can be destroyed by sunlight.

Minotaurs

Minotaurs once roamed the southern islands of Greece, particularly Crete. They were carnivorous, terrorizing isolated villages into making human sacrifices to appease them. Each had the body of a very strong and muscular man but the head and horns of a bull. They would let out a tremendous roar, which transfixed their victims to the spot with fear.

There is a tale of a king who constructed a complex labyrinth and placed a savage minotaur at its center, sending those who displeased him in to meet their death. It is said that a Greek hero called Theseus slayed the terrible demon. He solved the problem of the labyrinth by using a ball of thread, one end of which he tied to a post at the entrance, unraveling the ball as he proceeded. Once he had slain the minotaur, all he had to do was follow the thread back to the entrance.

As no reports of sightings have been made for at least two centuries, minotaurs are now presumed to be extinct.

Cyclops

These demons take the shape of one-eyed carnivorous giants who feed upon sheep and other livestock, considering mountain goats a great delicacy. They are found in the accounts of the early Greek historians and storytellers. It is possible that they are now extinct in that land, but there is some evidence that they have migrated north—there are records of sightings in southern Romania. In my opinion all accounts of "giants" are greatly exaggerated. No doubt there are humans and other creatures in this world that exceed normal dimensions, but the capacity of the human mind to embellish and exaggerate what already is a wonder in itself never ceases to amaze me.

A Cyclops

A Skelt

WATER BEASTS

Water beasts are to be found all over the known world in seas, lakes, rivers, marshes, ponds, and canals. In the County they cause the biggest problems north of Caster. It is my hope that one day I will train an apprentice who will specialize in dealing with such creatures.*

Scylla

Scylla are a type of fierce water beast to be found only in freshwater rivers and lakes in Greece. The creatures vary in size, but each of them has seven heads, two tails, and five limbs. Covered in green scales, they often hide in underwater foliage, then scuttle out at great speed

* At last I have trained an apprentice from that northern region of the County who wishes to return there and deal with things that come out of the water. His name is Bill Arkwright. —John Gregory

A Scylla

to seize their prey—usually fishermen or unwary travelers. The first scylla is said to have been one of the children of the first Lamia. It inherited its mother's voracious appetite, which has been passed down to her descendants.

Skelts*

Skelts resemble huge insects, with long, thin, multi-jointed legs. Despite their size, they can fold themselves into very narrow spaces. Their segmented bodies are hard and ridged like a crustacean and usually barnacle encrusted. They live close to water, often in caves, and emerge to feed on the warm blood of mammals. They have snouts but are toothless, and their most notable feature is a long, narrow, sharp bone tube, which they insert into their prey in order to suck its blood.

* Skelts are extremely rare. One day I hope to see one! —apprentice Bill Arkwright

Bill Arkwright got his wish! He had one trapped in a water pit below the mill. When it escaped, it attacked me and started draining my blood. Bill saved me, killing it with a rock. When he was a prisoner of water witches, they used a skelt to drink his blood. Once he was dead, the creature would have been ritually slain.
—Tom Ward

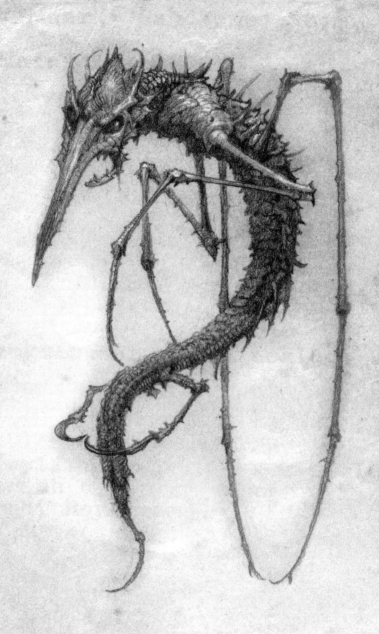

A Skelt

A Water Witch Feasting on a Skelt

where they are drowned, or sail their boats onto the rocks.* It is believed that sirens feed upon the flesh of the drowned.

A Wight

Wights

A wight is another creature created and used by witches, usually as the watery guardian of some secret place.† Wights are created using dark magic. A drowned sailor's soul is bound to his body, which then does

---

* *On the Greek coast, the crew of our ship, the Celeste, suddenly found themselves in thrall to sirens who waited on a headland of jagged rocks. These creatures, because of the power of their song, appeared as great beauties. However, their true form was hideous, with huge fangs and swollen lips. As spooks, Tom Ward and I had some immunity to their allure, but only by pressing wax into the ears of the helmsman could we free him from their spell so that the ship could be steered to safety. — John Gregory*

† *A wight was used to guard the secret tunnel that led to Malkin Tower. It was slain by a lamia, which tore it to pieces. — Tom Ward*

The skelt is greatly prized by water witches, who use it in their rituals. They allow it to drink the blood of a sacrificial victim over a period of days. Once the victim is dead, the witches then dismember the skelt alive and eat it raw. This triples the power of the blood magic gained.

Sirens

These female creatures use their powerful, enchanting voices to lure sailors to their deaths. In trying to reach the sirens, the mariners either plunge into the sea,

A Siren

not decay but becomes bloated and extremely strong. Although blind, their eyes having been devoured by fishes, wights have keen hearing and can locate their victims while still submerged. A victim may be totally unaware that a wight lies in wait in nearby water. The attack, when it comes, is swift. The wight seizes its prey and drags it down into deep water, where it drowns while being slowly dismembered.

Wights, like the witches who create them, can be repulsed and hurt by a staff of rowan wood. With a silver chain, they can also be dragged out of the water and finished off with salt and iron.

A Wight

Wormes

* The word worme is spelled with an e to distinguish it from the common earthworm.
—apprentice George Eccles

Wormes* are dangerous creatures that range in size from that of a small dog to something as big as a house. Some have legs, most have tails, and all are vicious and bad tempered. Their bodies are sinuous and eel-like, but covered with tough green scales that are very difficult to penetrate with a blade. They have long jaws with a mouth full of fangs that can bite off a head or an arm in the twinkling of an eye. When on land, they can also spit a deadly poison that is quickly absorbed through the victim's skin, with fatal results. Some wormes have short stubby wings, and because steam often erupts from their jaws, they are sometimes mistakenly believed to be fire-breathing dragons.

Wormes

They are mainly water dwellers, and although they prefer deep lakes, they occasionally make do with a marsh or river. Wormes are rare in the County but are to be found in its most northerly regions, ranging from the lakes down almost as far as Caster.

When they catch humans, they invariably squeeze their prey to death before eating them, bones and all, leaving hardly a trace. Sometimes they even swallow the clothes and shoes. But with animals such as cattle, they just bite deeply and drain them of blood.

Wormes are dangerous creatures to approach and are best dealt with by two people attacking the creature simultaneously.*

* I faced a dangerous worme with Bill Arkwright. I helped to attract its attention while he stabbed it with his staff, then finished it off with his knife. Bill also demonstrated how a candle flame could be used to distract it. —Tom Ward

A Dragon

ELEMENTAL SPIRITS

As the name suggests, elemental spirits emerge from earth, water, air, or fire over a long period of time. The elements give birth to them, but they move only very slowly toward consciousness. It is in the early stage of their development that novice witches can use them to exert power; the older the spirit, the more aware it is. Once they have interacted with a fully fledged malevolent witch, their development is complete.

One plausible theory is that elemental spirits eventually evolve first into demons, then finally into gods. There is no hard evidence for this, but it does seem likely. Thus the Old Gods are the result of a long developing process, the final catalyst being their worship by humans.*

* There is some recent evidence to support this view. The Bane was once one of the Old Gods, worshipped by the Little People. At the time of its unfortunate liberation from the catacombs under Priestown Cathedral, where it had little human contact, it had the strength of a demon. Gradually it then began to grow in power. I'm convinced that, using terror, it would eventually have forced people to worship it in great numbers. It would have become a god once more. It was destroyed by my apprentice, Tom Ward, just in time. — John Gregory

Barghests

Barghests are earth spirits that take the form of a huge black dog with fiery eyes and enormous fangs. Usually artificially bound to a certain location, they draw their strength from human fear, something they have in common with ghasts and boggarts. They are used and controlled by some witches to guard their homes, or places where covens gather. A spook can deal with them using salt and iron, but they can be a great danger to ordinary folk, projecting waves of fear that can stop a heart or drive the susceptible insane.

A Barghest

Boogles

Boogles are elemental spirits of earth that frequent caves and tunnels. Most are harmless, but they naturally make miners very nervous. They take the form of grotesque shadows that move extremely slowly. Occasionally they whisper or sigh. (Tappers are a much greater threat—see page 210.)

Dragons

Dragons are mistakenly believed by many to be fire breathers with wings and talons. True dragons are very different. They are elemental spirits of the air, some so large they can coil themselves right round a big hill. They often sleep for centuries like that, covering it from foot to summit. They are invisible, so most people aren't even aware of them. The more sensitive may just shiver suddenly on a hot summer's day and think they're coming down with a cold. Big dragons are sluggish things. They don't move much, but if they do, it happens very slowly.

Their thought processes also seem slow, but that's because they experience time differently: A day seems of no more duration than a second. Thus to them humans are no more than tiny insects and they are hardly aware of our existence. In ancient times, spooks could communicate with such beings, but that art has been lost.

Some mages try to use the energy of a dragon—with mixed results. There is great danger in such attempts. The mage is sometimes trapped within the aura of the dragon and falls into a deep sleep from which he never awakes, the most famous example being Merlin (see page 147, under Mages) who, it is said, still sleeps within a dragon's lair and will do so until the end of the world.

Fire Elementals

No doubt the reduced danger was in part due to that, but we must not discount the recent arrival of these elementals through the portal. After reaching our world, denizens of the dark always need time to achieve their full strength.
—John Gregory

Fire elementals are not found in the County because of its wet climate and prevailing westerly winds from the sea.* In hot lands, however, they can be very dangerous, often taking the form of glowing orbs, some of which are translucent, others opaque. At noon they are usually to be found on rocks, from which they draw heat and power. Additionally, they may frequent ruined or abandoned buildings.

As a general rule, the opaque ones are hotter and more dangerous than translucent ones. Indoors these often float close to the ceiling but can move very suddenly, which makes them almost impossible to dodge. Contact with such a sphere can result in severe burns and a painful death. In more extreme cases, such elementals can reduce their victims to ashes almost instantly.

Other fire elementals called asteri are similar in shape to a starfish, with five fiery arms. These elementals cling to the surface of walls or ceilings and drop onto the heads of unsuspecting victims.

The most dangerous fire elemental of all is the salamander, a large lizard that basks in the heat of intense flames. These can spit streaks of fire or scalding steam.

A Salamander

Fire elementals are notoriously difficult to defend against, but a metal alloy blade with the correct percentage of silver can sometimes cause one to implode. A spook's staff is particularly useful for this purpose.* Failing that, water can seriously weaken a fire elemental and cause it to hibernate until drier conditions prevail.† Water also offers a refuge when under attack.

Moroi

These are vampiric elemental spirits found in Romania. They are sometimes controlled by the strigoi and strigoica, but even when operating alone are a considerable threat to travelers. In their disembodied form, they inhabit hollow trees and clumps of holly. However, they often possess bears, which crush and lacerate their human victims before dragging them back to their lair. Sunlight destroys them, and they are only at large after dark.

* This proved to be the case when we were in Greece and encountered fire elementals. One of the asteri was cut in two by my staff's blade, but it was not the end of the elemental. It began to re-form, and we had to leave the location quickly. — John Gregory

† During our encounter with the Ordeen, a tremendous amount of water had fallen into the Ord, and this made some of the fire elementals less dangerous. —Tom Ward

Moroi have one significant weakness: They are compulsive in their behavior and often linger close to their lair, counting holly berries, seeds, twigs, or even blades of grass, wasting the hours that would otherwise have been used to hunt human prey. By the time they have finished counting, it's usually almost dawn—which can be the most dangerous time of all for unwary humans, because the creatures are desperate to drink blood before the sun rises.

This weakness is exploited by Romanian spooks, who always have a pocketful of seeds or berries. Threatened by the moroi, they cast these toward it. Rather than attack, it is forced to begin counting again.

Tappers

Tappers, distant cousins to the boggarts that plague the County, live deep within rock clefts and sometimes cause tunnels to collapse. County miners fear them more than anything else.

Tappers try to drive humans away from territory they have claimed as their own. First of all, they use fear—hence the mysterious and unnerving rhythmical tapping sounds that are typical signs of their presence. But if fear doesn't work, they bring down rocks and try to crush those they consider to be interlopers.

In an abandoned mine, huge numbers may gather unchecked over time, endangering the lives of any humans who venture there. Even many of them working together cannot cause a tunnel to collapse unless there is an existing fault line. However, if they do find a serious crack in the structure of the rock above, they can easily bring the ceiling down, either crushing or sealing victims underground so they perish from lack of air or water.*

* In a cave in the Pindhos Mountains, fleeing from maenads, Alice and I heard tappers all around us. They brought the roof down, and we only just escaped with our lives. —Tom Ward

Water Elementals

Water elementals are mostly found in the north of the County, where the bogs, lakes, and coast are inhabited by other denizens of the dark, such as water witches. There is a dangerous type called a wisp, which appears as a spiral of light over dangerous marshes and lures travelers off the path to their doom. These are usually too elusive to be dealt with unless there is a severe drought (a rare thing in the County). Then a spook can bind one in a pit using the same method as he would for a boggart.

A Wisp

Then there are banshees (also known as bean sidhe), which are female water spirits that warn of death. Mostly they are invisible: All you hear is a wailing cry, uttered just three times each night. If they are heard close to a house three nights running, it is said someone inside will die at the very moment the final wail is heard.

Sometimes banshees can be glimpsed apparently washing a burial shroud. If there is blood either on the shroud or in the water, then a violent death is predicted.* They are not solid and do not leave footprints or any other evidence of their presence.

A spook has no means of dealing with banshees, but they react to future events rather than bringing them about, so are not in themselves dangerous.†

* The predicted deaths do not always occur, leading me to suspect that coincidence may be involved, or that people simply die of fear, thereby fulfilling the prophecy. — John Gregory

† They are not to be confused with the Celtic witches (also known as banshee witches). These mimic the action of a banshee but actually bring about the death of their chosen victim. These witches worship the Old Goddess known as the Morrigan, who often appears in the shape of a crow. — John Gregory

A Banshee

The Cawley Stone Crawler

MYSTERIOUS DEATHS IN THE COUNTY

Spooks catalog the creatures of the dark. Bit by bit, year by year, we learn more about the threats posed by the dark and develop ways in which to thwart or limit its effects. But there are still entities out there that defy our attempts to take their measure. In the County there have been many mysterious deaths that so far have not been explained.

THE BLOATED BODY OF EMILY JANE HUDSON

Emily Jane Hudson had lived in Ormskirk all her life but had taken to her sick bed two years before her plight was brought to my notice. Doctors had visited her regularly, attempting unsuccessfully to deal with her strange affliction.

Emily was still alive when I first saw her. I had been called to her bedside by Dr. Gill, with whom I'd worked many times in the past; he was a liberal and intelligent man who understood

the part played in the County by the servants of the dark and
routinely sought my advice.

At first I thought I was dealing with a woman who was
extremely obese, but when the doctor lit a candle and pulled back
the bedclothes slightly, I was astonished by the sight of poor
Emily. Her face, shoulders, and neck were terribly swollen, but
there was not an ounce of visible fat on her. The bright red skin
was stretched tight by the blood beneath it. It was as if someone
or something had forced blood into the space between skin and
flesh. To support that theory, there were two large puncture
marks on her neck, and the same on each shoulder.

There are many cases in the County where blood has been removed from a living body. Witches who use blood magic do so routinely. Sometimes they drain their victim completely; at other times they draw blood in small amounts over days or even weeks. But never had I encountered a case where blood had been added rather than subtracted.

I was unable to help, and within two hours poor Emily was dead. Fortunately the local priest allowed her to be buried within the churchyard, which was of some consolation to her family.

Thus I was forced to record one more mysterious death in the County. I can only suppose that some unknown type of witch or dark entity was using her body as a place to store blood for some future ritual. But although I watched over her grave for weeks, they never returned to take it.

THE CAWLEY STONE CRAWLER

There have been many mysterious deaths near the outcrop of rock known as the Cawley Stone. At first it was animals being killed: sheep, rabbits, stoats, and squirrels. But twice I have been called to the area to investigate human deaths. The first was that of a hermit who lived in the woods nearby; the second time I traveled to view the remains of a shepherd who had pursued a stray lamb into the vicinity of the rock.

Both the lamb and shepherd were dead, but they had no

marks on their bodies—not even the slightest sign of violence.

The Cawley Stone has one visible peculiarity. About six feet from the ground on its northern face, there is a shape that might be a carving carried out in the distant past. If so, it has been weathered and worn and the details are not sharp. Alternatively, the shape could be the result of natural erosion. Whatever the truth of the matter, it has the appearance of a head, with muscular shoulders, arms, and hands. In certain lights, particularly just before sunset, it appears to be climbing out of the rock. If so, let us hope that it never completes its slow escape, because there is something very frightening about the figure.*

Some say that it is indeed emerging very slowly and claim to remember a time when it had not climbed out as far. Human memory is fallible, so we must allow for that, but I happened to speak to Jonathan Brown, the oldest resident of the nearby village. He says that as a young man he approached the Cawley Stone crawler for a dare and spent some time examining it closely. He was an artist who specialized in drawing landscapes and landmarks such as churches, so he took the opportunity to make a sketch of what he saw, striving, as usual, for accuracy. That sketch was still in his possession after all those years, and he showed it to me.

* I passed by the Cawley Stone just before sunset with my master, John Gregory, and we examined the crawler. It did appear to be climbing out of the rock and looked very scary indeed. I noticed that while we were there, everything was very still; there wasn't a breath of wind and the birds had stopped singing.—apprentice Henry Burrows

In the drawing, the figure was much further embedded in the rock: only one hand had emerged. I looked at some of his other work and was impressed by his eye for detail—particularly in his sketch of the gargoyle of the Bane, which is located over the main entrance to Priestown Cathedral. I was satisfied that he had rendered the crawler accurately—as it was then!

My suspicion is that we are dealing with some new type of earth elemental. It might well be that the rock face was worshipped in ancient times, sacrificial blood being splattered against it. That would have awakened the elemental, giving it strength and a sense of self. How it kills those who venture close, I do not know. But it is something to be aware of as it makes its slow escape from its rocky prison.

It may not need my attention again, but no doubt some future spook will be forced to deal with it.

THE MYSTERY OF THE CREEPING VINE

Late in the August of my fiftieth year, I was called from my
Chipenden home to view a death that defied explanation.

A suspected witch, Agatha Anderton, had long been watched at a
distance by wary and distrustful neighbors. I'd talked to her once
and found no evidence to support their whispered accusations.
Although advanced in years, Agatha was bright, alert, and in my
opinion, completely without malice—definitely falling into the
category of witch known as the falsely accused.

This final time I was summoned because of the state of
her house and garden. The latter had been overrun by a strange
yellow vine that had displaced her herbs and flowers; worse,
and far more ominously, it had grown over the exterior of her
cottage, covering walls, doors and windows in a profusion of
sickly smelling bloodred blossoms. No smoke had come from
her chimney for days, and her neighbors believed that witchcraft
was involved.

The vine was tough. Although it looked like fresh growth,
the stems were woody and I had to use an ax to cut it away from
the front door. Once inside, although it was just before noon, I
was forced to light a lantern because the rooms were so dark. I
gasped in shock, finding it difficult to believe my eyes.

The vine had apparently sprouted directly from poor
Agatha's body before displacing the floorboards and
splitting the wooden bed upon which the old

woman lay. She was cold and dead and had been in that condition for some time; her corpse was severely decayed.

But the real horror lay in what the vine had done to her body. Buds erupted from her dead flesh; shoots sprang from her ears and eyes; tendrils snaked down her nostrils and coiled about her throat; her feet and hands were covered in red blooms. The creeping vine had used her body as its soil, a nutrient to sustain its prolific growth.

Though it was hard to cut her from the bed, it had to be done. A priest was called, but although he said a few prayers over the body, he would not allow her to be buried in holy ground. So with his grudging permission, I laid her to rest just outside the churchyard.

From her grave the vine continued to sprout—but far more slowly than previously. Nevertheless, it's a dense, tangled growth from which both animals and humans keep their distance. After many years, it now covers a roughly circular area of approximately one hundred yards in diameter. I say circular, but it has extended in every direction but one; it has halted at the boundaries of the churchyard, almost encircling it but seemingly unable to encroach upon holy ground.

Why did it happen? It must remain one of the great mysteries of the County. I have no doubt that dark forces were involved. But whether it was conjured by Agatha Anderton or by some unidentified enemy, we will never know. If dark magic was used, it is a spell unknown to the witches of the County, suggesting that an incomer was involved.

Final Words

This Bestiary, my personal guide to the dark, is the last remaining book from the old spooks' library.

It is hard for me to convey the sense of loss I felt when the Chipenden library was destroyed. Up in flames went words written by generations of spooks, a great store of knowledge, the heritage of countless years of struggle against the ever-growing power of the dark. I was its guardian, and it was my task to extend and preserve it for the future. And now it is gone.

Its destruction filled me with a great sense of personal failure. It was a terrible blow that literally brought me to my knees.

Now I have had time to reflect, and I am filled with renewed strength and determination. My fight against the dark will continue. One day I will rebuild the library, and this book, my personal Bestiary, will be the first to be placed upon its shelves.

John Gregory

of Chipenden

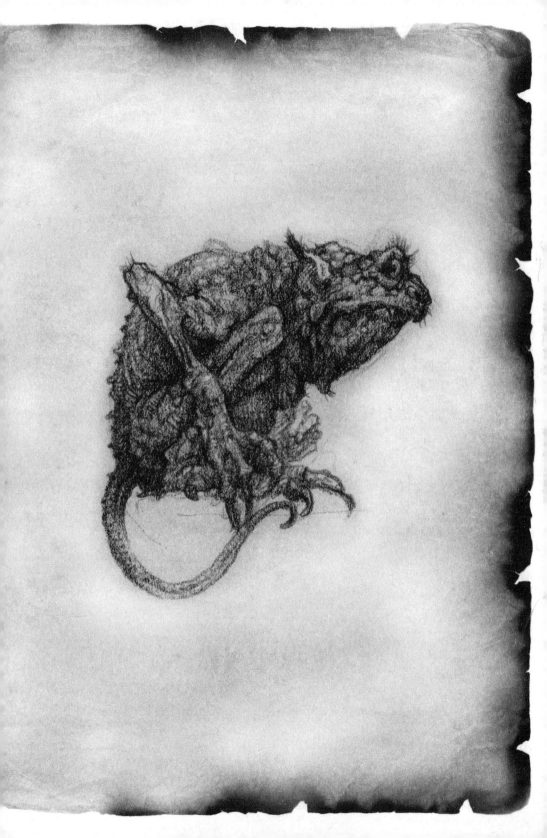

JOSEPH DELANEY lives in Lancashire and has three children and seven grandchildren. His home is in the middle of boggart territory, and his village has a boggart called the Hall Knocker, which was laid to rest under the step of a house near the church.

JULEK HELLER has been creating acclaimed fantasy illustrations for more than thirty-five years. His work appears in books such as *The Chronicles of Narnia, Giants,* and *The Mammoth Book of Arthurian Legends*. He also provides concepts and visualizations for film, television, and theater. Julek Heller lives with his family in London.